# MISTLETOE AND MAYHEM

## PORT DANBY COZY MYSTERY #3

## LONDON LOVETT

**Mistletoe and Mayhem**

Copyright © 2017 by London Lovett

ISBN-13: 978-1979434737

ISBN-10: 1979434735

# CHAPTER 1

*P*ort Danby was a picturesque little town on any given day, but covered in snow, it was nothing short of idyllic. The shops along Harbor Lane, including my own, Pink's Flowers, reminded me of cakes that had been decked out in colorful fondant and frosted with dollops of sugary white whipped cream. The town council and mayor had spared no expense in decorating the down-town area with holiday festoons. Long chains of remarkably real looking evergreen garland had been strung between the street lights. Large gold and red bells dangled from the garland, lending a true holiday spirit and the occasional tinny clang to the festive ambience.

The place felt magical during the day with the rainbow of colors and frenzied bustle of a town getting ready for Christmas, but at night, when the glittery lights on the rooftops, wharf and lighthouse reflected off the snow and the coastline, it felt as if Port Danby had been transported back in time to an old holiday classic like *A Christmas Carol* or *The Nutcracker Ballet*. It seemed at any moment the Sugarplum Fairies would emerge from the shadows and twirl along the sidewalks in candy pink tutus. The entire scene evoked a feeling of nostalgia and joy that was neatly wrapped by a ribbon of romance.

The morning sun sparkled off the lush mounds of feathery ice crystals piled on the awnings and window ledges as I walked along the sidewalk to my flower shop. Yes, the fallen flakes brought with them the occasional icy puddle or slippery square of sidewalk, but it was nothing compared to the inconveniences of snow in the big city. I surely never missed those days of trudging through gray slushy ice to catch a bus or a changing street light.

Ryder, my assistant, was leaning into the front bay window of the shop as I stepped inside. I began my ten minute un-layering ritual by removing my gloves and scarf.

Ryder straightened to see who had entered. "I thought you were going to take the morning off, boss," Ryder said. He had taken on the habit of calling me boss, and I found I didn't mind. It was all done with humor and respect. And it was my first time being a boss, so I was rather enjoying the sound of it.

"I've just got too much to do. I need to place some orders for the holiday table centerpieces."

Ryder pushed his long dark bangs away from his eyes, something he did a thousand times a day and yet he never considered changing his hairstyle. I couldn't blame him. The semi-edgy, semi-schoolboy haircut fit him perfectly. Ryder Kirkland was of average height and size, but there wasn't anything else average about him. He had just celebrated his twenty-fourth birthday, but was quite mature. He had been so perfect for my assistant florist position that sometimes it seemed I'd just dreamt him up and he popped off the job search website.

Ryder, with his playful smile, big blue puppy dog eyes had already endeared himself to all the other shop owners. He was polite, smart and he had a great sense of humor. And, aside from playing many instruments, Ryder was a walking encyclopedia. He knew copious details on a wide range of subjects, most especially plants due to his horticulture degree. He had also minored in fine arts, which gave him an incredible eye for design and color. Ryder had moved back to his hometown of Chesterton after college. He was working at Pink's Flowers so he could save up and travel the world to study exotic plants. I was thrilled and lucky that my humble little shop had fit into his future plans.

Ryder circled around the work island and grabbed a pair of scissors. "Where's Kingston?" To add to his list of perfect traits, Ryder was also a big fan of my pet crow, and the feeling was mutual. Kingston tended to always hang around the work station when Ryder was making arrangements or potting plants. Not everyone warmed up to having a big black crow standing watch while they worked, but Ryder thought it was cool.

"It was too cold for Kingston this morning. I pulled the cover off his cage, and instead of his usual dance, he tucked his beak back under his wing like a little kid pulling the covers back over his head. Birds and winter just don't mix unless the bird is a penguin."

Ryder clapped his hands together in one sharp smack. "Penguins! That's it. That's the color element I needed for the front window display."

"I hardly think of penguins as a color element but then you're the fine arts major. And I have no doubt that the holiday window display you create will win first place. But I have to remind you that the judging is just a few days away."

Port Danby was the final stop for the annual Harbor Holiday Lights Flotilla, a parade of festively decorated boats that made its way down the coastline every year. The town council had decided to hold a Port Danby window decorating contest to lend some spirit to the event. It was my first winter in my new town, and by all accounts, the floating light display was not to be missed. Apparently the yearly event attracted a huge crowd.

Head councilwoman and non-stop dynamo, Yolanda Petri, had come up with the contest idea, hoping the added holiday decor would make Port Danby stand out amongst the other coastal towns. As far as I was concerned, it already did. Still, I thought the contest was a great idea. Especially since my assistant had decided to make it his project, relieving me of the stress of coming up with something awesome enough to compete with the adorable gingerbread village my baking neighbor and friend, Elsie, had been constructing since the official contest announcement.

I hung up my coat and scarf on the hook next to the ribbon spools.

"Don't worry, boss, I've got it all covered." Ryder moved his jaw side to side in thought. "I wonder if they have any black sunflower seeds at the feed store in Chesterton. They're cheaper and bigger than chia seeds."

"Black sunflower seeds? For a holiday display?"

"For the penguins."

I reached down to lift up the box of mistletoe I'd purchased for a store freebie. I planned to tie up small clusters with red and blue ribbon and hand them to customers on their way out. "Sounds interesting but how will you keep a *certain bird* from eating the penguin made of seeds?"

Ryder's shoulders slumped. I felt bad for erasing his enthusiasm, but it was better of me to bring it up now instead of after he'd spent hours creating a seed covered display only to have it devoured by my crow.

"I'd forgotten all about Kingston. I guess black sunflower seeds would be too tempting. Let me give it some thought."

"Or I could always leave Kingston home for a few days," I suggested. "Not sure how Nevermore would feel about it but then I've been reminding myself lately that I need to seize control of the house back from my cat. Yesterday, Nevermore decided he was tired of watching me work on my computer, and without warning, he just hopped up onto the keyboard and sat down. My spread sheets looked like a Picasso painting. I yelled at him, but he just stared back with those big amber eyes and started licking his paw."

Ryder shook his head with a laugh. He began helping me pull apart the stems of mistletoe. "Sounds familiar. My mom rearranged all the living room furniture so that the couch was positioned to see out to the front yard and into the kitchen. She claimed her twenty pound tabby cat, Cooper, was sending her subliminal signals about furniture placement. Cooper likes to stretch out on the back of the couch. Now he can keep one eye on the birds playing on the lawn and the other eye on the can opener, the magical tool that somehow provides him with his food."

I started cutting the red and blue ribbon to tie the sprigs together. "I'm glad I'm not the only person hearing subliminal cat messages." I lowered the scissors for a second. "You know what, Ryder? You go on with whatever your plans are for the window. Kingston can stay home for a few days. It's too cold for him anyhow, and the trees lining Harbor Lane are covered in ice instead of leaves. He doesn't have any good place to perch. Not only that, but most of the smaller song birds have left town for warmer climates, so he doesn't have anyone to harass."

Ryder wore a permanent smile, but it grew bigger. "You're sure?"

"Yes. Go for it."

"Awesome." Ryder held up a stem of mistletoe. "Dung on a twig," he quipped. "That's what the word 'mistletoe' means. Birds and animals leave droppings nearby because they like to use the mistletoe for shelter."

"I've never heard that. Sort of dulls the shine on the kissing tradition."

"It's not just the name. It's kind of strange thinking that a parasitic plant like this became known for stealing kisses. Back in the early nineteenth century, they hung a type of mistletoe that had sticky white berries. They pulled a berry off with each kiss. Once the berries were gone, the kiss power was gone too. I noticed some of the bare ash trees behind the mayor's office had big basket shaped growths of mistletoe. They call them witches' brooms, although they hardly look like brooms. Is that where you got these?"

I titled my head at him. "Those trees are thirty feet tall. It was much easier and less precarious, albeit less adventurous, to have a delivery man bring them to the door."

Ryder pushed aside his bangs. "Makes sense. Besides, you might have upset a hawk's nest. I hear they like to use mistletoe to lay their eggs."

"So that was a win-win. The hawks keep their eggs, and I keep all my bones in place." I swept the ribbon pieces into a pile. "I'm going to draw up a chalkboard sign letting customers know they get free mistletoe with a purchase. Maybe you can draw a nice set of lips with some pink chalk at the top."

"I can do that. I studied lips a lot in college, both in art class and out," he added with a laugh. "Then I'd better get started on that window. Otherwise, it's going to be empty when the judge strolls by."

# CHAPTER 2

The bell on the door rang. Lola burst into the shop swinging around a picture of something. "Clearly, I am not a multi-tasker," she claimed confidently.

I continued with my chalkboard advertisement as she hopped up on the stool behind my work island.

"I was sitting at my computer, where I had a glue stick for pasting together a new flyer for the store. I also had a Chap Stick next to my keyboard because this cold, dry weather is turning my lips into red hot flames. Guess which one I used on my mouth?" Before I could laugh out my answer, she continued. "I'll give you a clue. As I walked out of the shop, Kate Upton walked past in a cashmere sweater, and a few of the hairs blew off and stuck to my lips."

A deep laugh rumbled from the bay window.

Lola spun around and glanced briefly at Ryder. "Hey, Ryder, didn't see you there."

"Morning, Lola," he called back energetically.

Lola's greeting ended. She turned back to me. Since I'd hired my new assistant, I'd learned something about my best friend, Lola. She was in constant pursuit of a steady relationship, and she was undeniably boy crazy. As long as that boy wasn't crazy about her. Lola had formed an instant crush on my new assistant before he'd even started working at the shop, but the second Ryder returned the interest, Lola's crush ended. Apparently Lola was more interested in the chase than the actual relationship. I felt bad for Ryder because he always looked a little lovelorn after seeing Lola. And I was a bit aggravated with my friend because she was passing up a prime opportunity. Of course, it was probably just as well that my best friend and shop assistant weren't involved. I'd be stuck in the middle and that was never a good position.

I stepped back and admired my sign. It just needed a pair of lips to really draw attention from people passing by. I'd noticed that with the winter cold penetrating every corner of town, pedestrians tended to walk with their faces down and tucked halfway behind thick collars or deep hoods to avoid the glacial air. It took more effort to attract them into the store. I was sure free mistletoe and the promise of stolen kisses would be the perfect lure.

"Why are you giving the mistletoe away for free?" Lola asked. "Tom and Gigi are charging a dollar a bag down at the Corner Market."

My entire body deflated with disappointment. "They are? Why are they selling it at all? They are a food market."

Ryder heard the turn in topic and climbed out of the window.

"It's their most popular item this time of year," Lola said with a shrug. "The high school kids buy up the baggies faster than Gigi can package the stuff. And, except for the baggies, it's all profit. Tom climbs up into the ash trees behind the mayor's office and cuts the sprigs himself. Although, last year there was an incident with a nesting hawk, so his supply line got cut short."

Ryder and I exchanged amused looks. "Well, your mistletoe is free," Ryder noted, looking for a bright spot.

"Yes, with a purchase," I added. "And I don't want Gigi and Tom to be upset. Maybe I need to cancel the whole idea." I ran my palm over the pile of cellophane wrapped mistletoe. "But what on earth will I do with all this—what did you call it?" I asked Ryder. "Dung on a twig?"

That comment earned a burst of laughter from Lola, but she quickly stifled it with her hand when she saw that I was truly in a bind. Ryder was just about to make a suggestion when Lola spoke past him.

"I've got a brilliant idea!" She grabbed the picture she'd carried into the shop. "I was just on my way over here to ask you to make me a Victorian kissing bough for my window display. I was in the store-room pulling out all the old Victorian toys and I found this."

She pushed the picture into my hands, and Ryder circled around to look over my shoulder. The picture was a pencil drawing of a scene inside a tavern or some other public gathering place. A round bellied man in knee length breeches, buckled shoes and a John Bull topper was clutching a woman draped in a frilly fichu and flouncy mob cap. His mouth was pursed for a kiss, but the woman looked less than happy about the prospect. Hanging above them was a round ball decorated in holly leaves, ribbon and fruit. A cluster of mistletoe hung from the base of the sphere.

I'd seen Victorian kissing boughs or balls in pictures, but I'd certainly never tried to create one. "I don't know, Lola. It looks complicated."

"The English have been making these boughs since the medieval times. They became very popular in the nineteenth century." Ryder took hold of the picture to get a closer look. "All we need is some wire and the greenery to wrap around it. I don't think it would be too hard. We could even make a few for you to sell in the shop. You might even start a new tradition here in town."

Lola nodded her approval at Ryder's suggestion. He had to tamp down his smile. I think Ryder was figuring out the game and was deciding to remain aloof when it came to Lola.

Lola hopped off the stool. "So, it's settled. A kissing bough is the perfect finishing detail for my window. Not that I'll win. Have you seen Elsie's gingerbread town? When does that woman sleep or eat or live? When she isn't baking, she's running through town, and the snow hasn't slowed her at all. When I'm her age, I hope I have half of her energy. Heck, I wish I had it now." Lola stopped with her rant about Elsie and glanced toward the big front window. Ryder had stripped it bare. "Pink, you better get started on that window display. You're running out of time."

"I've got it under control," Ryder said. "Prepare to be awestruck."

Lola raised a brow at him. "If you say so." She didn't notice how her curt response crumpled his posture a bit. Sometimes, I just wanted to give her a little shake. "Well, I should get back to my own window. Not sure how I feel about this whole thing. I've got so much to do, yet I'm spending time pulling moth eaten toys out of the storeroom. Some of them are covered with spider webs, and I hate spiders." She headed to the door. "The boats are starting to roll into the harbor," she said as she opened the door. "Do you want to grab some lunch later and walk down to see them?"

"Sure," I said. "Just as soon as I figure out how to construct a Victorian kissing bough."

# CHAPTER 3

*A* gray mist was hovering over the ocean, but that hadn't stopped seemingly everyone in town from walking down to the wharf to watch the boats sail in. It was midday so there were no dazzling light displays yet, and most of the boats had secured or removed their decorations for the trip from Mayfield Bay to Port Danby. It was probably a wise precaution. The water along the marina looked particularly murky and restless this afternoon. Even the boats already moored in the slips were beating out a rhythmic tune as their hulls drummed against the pier.

One thing I hadn't gotten used to was the incongruous scene of snow piled along a beach. Icy drifts seemed out of place in the midst of an ocean port, yet the white caps on the pylons and the bows of the rusty fishing boats made me smile. One boat owner had even sculpted a miniature snowman to sit proudly at the stern. A captain's hat had been placed at a jaunty angle on the snowman's head and shells had been used for eyes and a nose.

Cold as it was out on the wharf, Lola had insisted on buying a chocolate covered ice cream bar for the walk. She stopped suddenly and stared down in despair at a sizeable piece of chocolate shell that had broken free. "Oh man, I hate it when that happens. The chocolate is the best part."

"I believe that is a sentence that can be used in almost any context." I pointed to the large wooden gingerbread men standing hand in hand along the planks of the pier. "I hadn't seen the row of gingerbread people. They must be new." In preparation for the holiday light flotilla, an event that was even going to draw in news crews on Saturday night, the town had decided to decorate the entire marina. Pickford Marina consisted of a long wharf where fishermen could clean their catch and visitors could rent a bike or stop for a shrimp salad. A long set of parallel docks ran adjacent to the wharf. The various slips were filled with every size and shape of pleasure boat. Farther out were the larger slips for fishing boats and the occasional visiting yacht. The boats that had come to town for the holiday flotilla would be anchored off Pickford Beach, where us landlubbers could view them from the wharf or the sand.

"They put those gingerbread men up every year," Lola said over a bite of ice cream. "I guess someone finally took the time to repaint them. They were starting to look a little shabby." She elbowed me. "Look who Yolanda has once again lassoed into helping with the lights."

I gazed down to the end of the wharf where my tall, charming and unmistakably handsome neighbor, Dash, was hanging a wreath on a light pole.

"I'm not too surprised he's helping. Dash told me this was his slowest time of year. Apparently, boat repairs and maintenance are not high priorities in winter. He gets really busy in spring though, before the season starts."

The chocolate was gone, so Lola tossed the rest of the ice cream into the trash can as we passed it. "I guess he's like the accountant who does taxes. I always wonder what they do from May to December. Of course, Dash would never look right sitting behind a desk, chewing on the end of a pencil and crunching numbers. Although, I'll bet he looks spectacular in a suit."

Dash noticed Lola and me walking along the pier. He waved. The tall ladder beneath him wobbled, but it didn't seem to faze him in the least.

"He sure spots you easily in a crowd," Lola noted.

I glanced around. At that moment, the only other people in the vicinity were the stoutly carved gingerbread people. "In this crowd? I sure hope so."

"Is it true that he got back together with Kate Upton after Thanksgiving?" Lola lowered her voice, but again, only gingerbread men were there to listen in on our conversation.

"I guess I didn't tell you—"

Lola stopped and turned to face me, her eyes wide with anticipation of possible juicy gossip. "No, you didn't. What? And don't leave out anything."

"There's not much to leave out, except Dash told me he ended up cancelling his first plans for Thanksgiving because his dad sprained his ankle on the golf course. He flew home to help out his parents."

"His first plans? You told me Kate had invited him to a reunion of their mutual friends."

"That's what Kate told me, but Dash wasn't any more specific than that. I can only assume he meant the dinner at Kate's."

"Interesting," Lola purred as we continued on our aimless journey.

"Not really, but whatever floats your boat. Pun intended."

Lola had an imaginary relationship in her head between Dash and me. As attractive and kind and chivalrous as my broad shouldered, blond haired neighbor was, there had been nothing between us aside from some intermittent flirting and several incidents where he came to my rescue. Including one where I fell literally into his arms.

For no other reason except we were both procrastinating from having to go back to work, we walked down the pier steps and headed out on the sand to view the boats.

Yolanda Petri had been so busy studying her clipboard, she nearly smacked into us as we stepped onto the beach. Yolanda was always hustling and hurrying. Even though I knew she was frazzled, not a hair was out of place on her short, neatly cut bob, and she even managed to keep the pleats in her jeans.

"Lacey, Lola, can you believe all these people on the beach? No one was supposed to show up until the light displays, but look at this place." She swept her arm around once. "Every busy body in the world is out here, which only makes it harder for those of us organizing the event." As she spun back to face us, the top paper on her clipboard flew away.

I bounded after it through the sand and managed to grab the corner with the toe of my boot. I picked it up and glanced at it. The Merry Carolers was typed across the top, and a list of names was printed below. The first name, Charlene Ruxley, caught my attention for no reason other than it was an unusual surname. I handed Yolanda the paper.

"Thank you, Lacey."

"You're welcome. So a group of carolers are going to be part of the festivities?"

Yolanda smiled proudly. "I was lucky to get them. They are highly sought after at this time of year. They've already arrived. They've parked their two motor homes at the Mayfield Bay campsite."

Lola was poking my arm trying to get my attention, but Yolanda wasn't through talking about the carolers.

"They'll be dressed in Victorian costumes. I've seen pictures. It's going to be so much fun. I've even hired a horse and carriage to give people rides through town. It'll be as if Port Danby has been transported back into a Charles Dickens novel," Yolanda continued on enthusiastically. But then her face fell slightly. "But without the cobblestone or thatched roofs or plum pudding."

"Or the cool British accents," Lola added unhelpfully, obviously not noticing that with each missing element Yolanda's vision was deflating like an old balloon.

I patted Yolanda's arm. "And without the charcoal choked fog and the sour face of Ebenezer Scrooge." And just as I finished the name, Mayor Price bellowed down to Yolanda from the pier, negating my second point. Just like his polyester suits, the mayor's overcoat was stretched to capacity over his round belly. His crooked moustache twitched below his bulbous nose as he motioned for Yolanda to join him. As always, he scowled when he saw me standing next to Yolanda. Then, as always, he looked up at the sky to see if he could catch my ornery pet doing something wrong. I was relieved that Kingston was at home.

"Oh dear," Yolanda muttered, "what does that man want now?"

I patted her arm again in sympathy. "You're doing a great job, Yolanda. We'll let you get back to it. Lola and I are just going to take a quick walk around, then we'll get out of the way."

Lola grabbed my arm as I started walking. "I've been trying to get your attention." She leaned closer. "Did you see who was standing down near the water, eating his burger and chatting with a boat owner?"

The mist was getting heavier, but I could see a familiar figure standing just a few feet from where the foamy water was sliding over the sand. Detective Briggs was wearing a black hat to keep his head warm. He had a thick coat on over his usual business-like attire. He was a man who looked as good in a suit as he looked in a sweater or t-shirt. We had spent a good deal of time together solving two different murder cases. Something that I found exhilarating, especially when my super sense of smell played a part in finding evidence. And, if I was being perfectly honest, I found working with Detective Briggs exceptionally nice. Naturally, Lola, who was obsessed with romance and who had an overactive imagination, had decided there was more to our friendship than the occasional murder mystery. I'd assured her many times that James Briggs was only interested in my sense of smell, slim medical knowledge and ability to connect dots in a murder case. Which was fine by me. When I left behind my high paying job in a perfumery, I also left behind a no-good scoundrel of a fiancé. Now I was an independent businesswoman and loving my freedom. The last thing I needed was to cloud my thoughts with a man.

And almost as if he'd read those thoughts, Detective James Briggs stepped out of the cloudy mist and stopped just a few feet in front of me.

"Detective Briggs," his name shot out after a quick inhale.

"Miss Pinkerton." The man seemed to know exactly how to smile to make me release a silent sigh.

It had been a few weeks since I'd been face to face with Detective Briggs, so it took me a second to notice the man behind him. He wasn't a local. He looked to be about forty with smoky gray sideburns and wavy black hair tucked under a dark blue captain's hat with the words Sea Gem embroidered in gold. I could only assume he had ferried to shore on one of the small row boats sitting on the sand.

Briggs pointed toward Pickford Way. "Mr. Ruxley, if you take this street east and turn left onto Harbor Lane, you'll see the Corner Market on your right."

"Thank you again, Detective Briggs." The man walked in the direction of Pickford Way.

"Is that man's name Ruxley?" I asked.

"Yes, Chad Ruxley. He owns that twenty foot sailing sloop sitting anchored just past the buoy. Why? Do you know him?"

I looked out to sea and saw that the words Ruxley Plumbing had been painted on a sign. Elsie had mentioned that the boat owners usually advertised their companies or took on advertisements to help pay for the cost of being a part of the flotilla. "No, it's just I saw that name on the carolers' list and I thought—what are the odds of hearing or seeing that unusual name twice in the same day."

Briggs nodded a polite hello to Lola, who had fallen silent. She stood back a few feet as if she was watching a show rather than standing in a three way conversation. Sometimes she was incredibly silly.

Briggs turned back to me. "Then I suppose the odds of seeing that name three times in the same day are even slimmer. There's another boat out there with the same name." Briggs pointed out to a pleasure boat that had a large holly wreath hanging up on the pilot house window. The sign posted said T. Ruxley Plumbing.

I looked back at Briggs confused. "Same company? Did they forget the T on the first boat?"

The three of us headed back to the steps.

"Apparently, they are two brothers who had a falling out some years back. They split up the company. So the second brother added a T to his company name," Briggs said.

"That has to be confusing," Lola finally spoke up.

"I'd say so." Briggs made sure not to look in the direction of Dash working on lights, and Dash seemed to make the same effort to avoid eye contact. I had yet to figure out what had happened between them, and I wasn't about to bring it up.

"I guess you've been busy," Briggs said as we reached the end of the pier. Lola continued on.

"Holiday season. Plus I had to train my new assistant. Not that it took much training. Ryder is such a solid help, I've got more spare time now. In fact, I'm planning to dive into that Hawksworth murder case later today. I'm going to the Chesterton Library just like you suggested. Of course, that also means I have time to help you solve some current crimes. If you need the help, that is." I tapped my nose. "Bridget and I are ready for action."

"Bridget?"

"What do you think of that nickname for my sniffer? Too kitschy?"

He laughed, and I realized it had been weeks since I'd heard it. "It's your nose. I suppose you can name it whatever you like. Have fun with the Hawksworth case, and let me know what you find. Oh, and Miss Pinkerton, I'll let you know if I need you and Bridget for a case."

"Yes, now that I hear you say it, I'm thinking it's too pretentious. And anytime!"

# CHAPTER 4

*I*'d left Ryder elbow deep in wire and chicken mesh. He had decided to keep the entire window display a secret, even from me. Although, I caught a glimpse of a five pound sack of black sunflower seeds so I could at least hazard a guess that there would be a penguin sitting in the display.

Ryder had used the same wire and chicken mesh to create a sphere shaped form for Lola's kissing bough. I knew exactly where some lush holly berry bushes grew alongside Culpepper Road, so the bough was a perfect excuse for me to take a trip to Chesterton Library. After seeing Detective Briggs earlier in the day, I had a terrible urge to immerse myself in a murder mystery. And since there had been no convenient murders lately, I had to go back in time to the century old Hawksworth family mystery.

Most of the morning's clammy mist had evaporated, and for the last hours of its arc through the sky, the sun was trying its hardest to warm the air. I pulled my car over and hopped out with my holly collecting supplies, a pair of pruning shears and a paper bag. The holly bushes were sprawling and wildly tangled. It seemed they'd been planted along Culpepper Road many years back and then left to fend for themselves. They'd fared pretty well, even withstanding the yearly blanket of snow.

I made quick work of my trimming errand and filled the bag with sprigs of holly and berry clusters. The Chesterton Library would be closed in an hour, and I wanted time to peruse the stacks of old newspapers they boasted about on their website.

I climbed back into the car and exchanged my wet gloves for dry ones before heading to Highway 48 and the town of Chesterton. By the time I'd parked in the small six car lot in front of the library, I had forty-five minutes for browsing.

The Chesterton Library looked like a house you'd see in any small neighborhood. It had been painted barn red, which was perfectly complimented by bright white window trim and shutters. The front door was painted dark blue with two sidelights. There was a metal bike rack positioned between two evergreen saplings. Both young trees were propped up by wooden poles to keep the ocean breeze from snapping their tender trunks.

I left my coat and gloves in the car, deciding I could bear the short walk to the door without them. I didn't want them in my way when I looked through the stacks. Various flyers advertising everything from the local Christmas tree farm to the holiday light flotilla had been pinned to the front of the wooden counter.

A young girl with a volunteer badge was sitting on the stool behind the check out desk. Her long tawny bangs covered her eyes as she stared down at her phone. She was surrounded with marvelous books, but she was honed in on her phone.

I cleared my throat, and she lifted her face. "We close in forty-three minutes." It seemed she had closing time down to the second. I could only assume the volunteer position was something her counselor had told her to do to beef up her college application.

"Yes, I'm aware of the time. Could you point me in the direction of the old newspaper stacks?"

She tilted her head. "I would have taken you more as a fiction reader, thrillers or maybe romance."

"And you'd be right on both accounts. Now, as you mentioned, there are only forty-three minutes until closing."

"Forty-two but who's counting."

"You, apparently. The newspapers?"

She leaned forward as far as she could without falling off the stool. "Through that door and to the left. But you'll have to ask Tilly before you go into the newspaper stacks."

Her last comment stopped my progress. "Tilly?"

"Tilly Stratton, head librarian. You can't miss her. She's wearing a Mrs. Claus apron. She just finished story hour in the kids area."

I followed the girl's directions and entered a large room that had been divided into different sections with tall bookshelves and strategically placed tables and chairs. White orb shaped pendant lights hung around the room, giving each section its own round, warm glow. A small corner of computers with a sign that said "For Homework Use Only" sat beneath a row of posters showing various famous authors, like Austen and Twain. Aside from two high school kids, who looked more interested in each other than in their math homework, the room was empty.

I turned around just as a middle aged woman with a bowl shaped haircut and front teeth that were a touch too long came out from an office. A bright red, ruffle covered apron with the words, "Mrs. Claus" embroidered in green silk floss across the front assured me I'd found the head librarian.

Tilly Stratton looked up at me through her round rimmed glasses as I approached the circulation desk. Her top lip slipped up when she smiled, making her front teeth even bigger. "May I help you?"

"Yes, thank you. I'm interested in looking at the Chesterton Gazette. I understand it was a paper that was circulated around Chesterton and the surrounding towns at the turn of the last century."

"It was indeed. They stopped the printing press on that paper just after World War I. People were no longer interested in only local news. I guess the war opened their eyes to the fact that there was a whole big world around them." She stepped out from behind a swinging gate and motioned for me to follow.

"I've never seen you here. Are you a local?" she asked as she led me through a door and down a short hallway.

"I moved to Port Danby in early fall. I have a flower shop in town. And now that I've seen how wonderful your library is, I think you'll see more of me." I could see her straighten her posture with pride as I complimented *her* library. I'd quickly decided it would be smart to get on her good side if I wanted to spend researching the Hawksworth case.

We entered a room that was dark until she flipped on a light. It wasn't as cozily decorated as the main library rooms, but there was a table and chairs in the center of the floor, which was made smaller by the rows of shelves lining every wall. Instantly, the smell of dry stale ink and yellowed, dusty paper filled my nose. The shelves and room swirled around me for a second as I worked to gain control of my sensitive nose.

Tilly stopped and tapped her chin. "Let me guess. You're interested in the Hawksworth murders."

My eyes rounded in surprise. "Why yes. How did you know?"

She headed to a particular set of shelves. "I get people in here all the time asking about it. Even your mayor." Her glasses bobbed up and down on her nose as she scrunched it. "What's his name?"

"Mayor Price."

"Yes, that's him. He used to come in here to browse the articles surrounding the case, but I haven't seen him in at least a year." She reached up to one of the shelves and pulled a pair of latex gloves out of a box. She handed them to me. "If you don't mind. The newspapers deteriorate faster if they get oily. The dates are on the front of the shelves. There are some pieces of notepaper and pencils on the table, but please don't write on the newspapers. I'm afraid you won't have more than thirty minutes though. We're closing up soon."

"Right. Thirty minutes. It'll be a good start." I pulled on the gloves. "Thank you."

My time was limited. Instead of heading for the obvious, the newspapers from October 1906, the month and year of the murders, I decided to skim through front page headlines from earlier dates just to get a sense of how important the Hawksworth family was at that time.

After wasting a good third of my precious short time in the newspaper room, I caught a glimpse of the name Hawksworth on the front page of the Chesterton Gazette. It was dated February 3, 1901, a good five years before the murders. The picture, which was somewhat unfocused to begin with, had both faded and yellowed with time. But the headline was clear. "Hawksworth Breaks Ground on Shipping Yard."

I carried the paper to the table and sat down to skim the article and get a closer look at the headline picture and the two small images beneath it. I put on my reading glasses. The article mentioned that after a three year battle with local and state government officials, the millionaire businessman and entrepreneur, Bertram Hawksworth, finally had a start date for his massive shipbuilding yard. The shipbuilding facility would stretch along two miles of the coast, ending just south of the Port Danby shipping lanes. At that time, Port Danby was still an important stop for merchant ships. Decades later, the port was deemed obsolete and lost business to the larger, more accessible ports farther south. My quaint new hometown, a popular tourist stop and coastal nook, would have looked much different if it had remained a shipping port.

I sat forward and leaned my face closer to the picture. I'd seen Bertram Hawksworth, looking severe and grim in several family portraits where he'd posed with a stone face to look like the typical somber Victorian man of the house. But this photo showed a much more jovial man. His bushy sideburns looked like giant fuzzy caterpillars lining each rounded cheek as he flashed a wide, proud grin for the camera. Another man stood nearby holding Bertram's black coat and top hat as Hawksworth, clad in his drop shoulder white shirt with sleeves rolled up, a look that was scandalously brazen back then even for a man, pushed a shovel into the ground. In the distance, the ocean curled over into crested waves. The photographer even managed to catch a seagull passing over the water. The jetty to the right of where the men were standing still stood today as a natural, rugged border between Mayfield and Port Danby. I'd been along that strip of beach more than once, and I didn't ever remember seeing a shipyard or even the remnants of something as large and industrial as a place big enough to build ships.

Tilly popped her face into the room. "Just wanted to give you a ten minute heads up. And please just leave any newspapers on the table. I prefer to shelve them myself. Otherwise, they get thrown into disarray."

"That's fine. I'm just finishing up."

She walked back out.

I moved my gaze down to the picture below the headliner. It was Bertram Hawksworth, dressed again in coat, dress shirt and ascot. He was sitting behind an intricately carved mahogany desk looking very important and almost presidential as he signed some documents with a nib pen. The caption read 'Mr. Bertram Hawksworth signing contractor documents for the Hawksworth Shipbuilding Yard'.

I glanced at the clock on the wall. My time was up. I certainly hadn't gleamed much information today, but I'd return when I had more time. I stood up and stared down at the picture as I pulled off the gloves.

"He signs with his left hand," I muttered into an empty room. There was nothing wrong with his right hand, as far as I could see. It sat there plain and empty on the desk as he signed the papers with his left. If Bertram Hawksworth was left-handed, then why did the grisly picture of the murder-suicide show him holding the gun in his right hand?

# CHAPTER 5

*B*y the time I reached the shop, the sun had set and the daytime fog had cleared into a navy blue night where the twinkling holiday lights nearly blotted out nature's twinkling lights in the sky above.

Ryder was still working on his window display when I got back to the shop. He was sitting on the floor with a large wire sculpture in front of him. I wasn't supposed to ask questions, but I was sure I saw a bear taking shape in the wire.

"You're still here, Ryder? You must be tired. Head home. I'm going to close up."

"I'm just finishing up one more part." One of Elsie's pink bakery boxes was sitting next to him on the floor with the twine curled into a pile and the lid open, exposing the last crumbs of a blueberry muffin and cupcake inside.

"Looks like you're fueled up with Elsie's goodies. I hope if I'm ever stuck on a deserted island that I end up there with a year's supply of Elsie's blueberry muffins. They are the perfect survival food."

"I agree," Ryder said without looking away from his project.

I dropped the bag of holly on the work island. "I've got the greenery for Lola's kissing bough. I'll work on it in the morning."

"Oh"—Ryder finally lowered the pliers he was holding—"that reminds me. Elsie said you should take a ride in the horse-drawn carriage. It's free for Port Danby shop owners tonight. The driver wants to get the horse used to the street before he starts taking on paying customers tomorrow night."

"Sounds like the shop owners are his guinea pigs."

Ryder laughed. "I did see the horse balk at the overhead bells once or twice, but the driver seems to know what he's doing. Elsie mentioned that his name is Gerald Tate, and he's the great-grand nephew of Marty Tate, the lighthouse keeper."

"Oh really? Then it seems I might meet the great-grand nephew before I meet the great uncle. I've been living in town since September, but I have yet to meet Marty Tate."

Ryder looked up in surprise. "Really? I guess it makes sense. I think his arthritis keeps him indoors a lot. When I was in elementary school, we used to take field trips to the lighthouse. Marty would give each of us a vanilla wafer and a postcard on the way back to the bus."

"That is so cute. We never had cool field trips like that. Although, in third grade we went to Burger King, and we all got to wear paper crowns and eat fries on the bus. That's all I remember about it." I grabbed a broom from the potting area and began sweeping up the remnants of mistletoe and other debris collecting on the floor.

"You might be in luck tonight. I saw Marty riding in the carriage when they brought Elsie back to the bakery. He was bundled up in a scarf, hat and thick coat as if he intended on riding around for awhile."

"That's great. I was going to head over to the police station. Maybe I'll take the carriage down there. Then I can finally meet Marty. I'm a big fan of the Pickford Lighthouse. It's one of the reasons I chose Port Danby for my new home."

Ryder leaned back on his hands and turned his head side to side to check out his sculpture.

"I know it's supposed to be a secret, but I see a bear," I said.

He sighed with relief. "That's good to know. I was starting to worry it looked more like a mouse." He pushed to his feet and picked up the tools. "Well, I'm heading out. I'm meeting some friends for dinner in Chesterton. The carriage stops and drops off just before the Mod Frock. He's making the rounds about every fifteen minutes." He cupped his ear. "In fact, I hear the clip-clop of horse hooves right now. I'll finish sweeping. You go catch the carriage."

An unbidden laugh rolled off my lips as I pictured myself waving it down like I used to do for a taxi in the city. "I will. But I'll sweep up tomorrow morning before we open. You go home and meet your friends."

Ryder walked to the hook on the wall and pulled off his coat and beanie. "Why are you going to the police station?"

"Nothing important. I've been scratching around looking for information about the Hawksworth murders, and I found something of interest to mention to Detective Briggs."

Ryder glanced toward the front window. "There's the carriage. You should hurry. I'll lock up on my way out."

"Thanks." I walked out to the sidewalk. One large, straw colored horse with a thick neck and billowy white mane and tail was steadily pounding the icy asphalt with its wide feet. The driver sat up tall and proud on the box seat of an open carriage in his black coat and top hat.

I hurried my pace and reached the sign that had been posted for carriage rides. Beginning tomorrow night, passengers would be paying ten dollars for the short trip down to the wharf. I was sure the man would have a booming business. Who would pass up the chance to ride in a horse-drawn carriage?

"Whoa, Mary, whoa," the driver said in a soothing tone. The horse's vision was blocked by the standard black blinders. A safety precaution, no doubt. Its bridle and head gear had been decorated with red ribbons, and the horse's mane, on closer inspection, had several rows of braids, also decorated with ribbon.

"Hello there," the driver called down. "Are you a shop owner?"

"Yes, I am. I'm Lacey Pinkerton of Pink's flowers." As I finished my introduction, the carriage waddled a bit and a passenger that I hadn't noticed leaned out past the driver's box.

Kind gray eyes peered out from the narrow opening below the hat and above the scarf that was piled up in front of his face. Gloved hands reached up and pulled the green scarf away from his nose and mouth.

"So I finally meet the flower shop girl." His voice was stuttering and weathered by the years, but I liked the sound of it.

"You must be Mr. Tate," I said excitedly. "I've been anxious to meet you."

"Then hop aboard." He lowered his hand out for me to take as I stepped up in to the carriage.

I dropped into the tufted red velvet cushions and immediately drew my coat in closer around me. "Mr. Tate, I just want to say that my favorite sight on this entire coast is your lovely lighthouse."

"Please, call me Marty." A gritty chuckle followed. "And I have to agree with you."

I leaned back against the comfortable seats and watched the stars and lights roll past. "This is a great way to travel. I feel like I'm looking at the town with a whole new set of eyes. If someone ever figures out time travel, I'm heading straight back to the horse and buggy era."

Marty laughed. "You'd get tired of it the second you discovered that there were no telephones or computers."

"You're right. That would be a big drawback."

"Dash tells me you live next to him on Loveland Terrace. My cousin Nina used to live in that house. That was years ago of course. There have been other families in there since."

"I couldn't have found a more charming home. And it has a great view of the town."

I could only see parts of his face, but it didn't look nearly as wrinkled as I'd expected. Maybe he wasn't as old as everyone purported him to be.

"What do you think of that old, decaying mansion behind you? Bet you have a pretty good view of that too. That house was the pride of the town back when it was built. I remember it looking elegant and stately when I was a boy."

Maybe the man just aged remarkably well.

I sat forward with interest. "Did you know the Hawksworth family?"

Even his grand nephew had a good laugh from that question.

"No, I'm not quite that old. Even though the house wasn't occupied, it took many years until it started to decay. It was an architectural masterpiece. It's a shame it became a relic and a reminder of a terrible event."

"I'm sorry. Of course, you couldn't have known them."

"Not to worry. My mother knew the family. She grew up in Port Danby. Stop by the lighthouse sometime, and I'll show you pictures of the town in the old days. I've even got pictures of the lighthouse under construction."

The carriage slowed as we reached the drop off place at the end of Harbor Lane.

"I will absolutely make time to do that. And I'm so glad we finally got to meet." I looked up at the driver as I climbed out. "And thank you for the ride. It was quite memorable."

I waved to Marty as the horse and carriage turned around and then I headed to the police station. I was in luck. Detective Briggs' car was still parked out front.

# CHAPTER 6

Officer Chinmoor and Hilda, the woman who ran dispatch, had gone home for the night. But the door to Detective Briggs' office was open, which meant he was technically manning the front desk. He heard the door shut and walked out to the front counter. He had the sleeves of his dress shirt rolled up, exposing a strong pair of forearms.

"Miss Pinkerton, didn't expect to see you." For one brief, glorious evening, when everyone came to my house for Thanksgiving dinner, Briggs let down his professional facade and called me Lacey. In turn, I had called him James. It had sounded perfectly right when I said it too. But after the mashed potatoes, yams and pies had been divided up for leftovers and the holiday had come to a successful end, he switched back to Miss Pinkerton. I was disappointed, but it made sense. He was, after all, head detective for a long stretch of coastline.

I fingered the plastic garland that Hilda had draped along the front of the counter. The police station was a bleak, dull place, but Hilda made subtle attempts to spruce it up for the holidays. Unfortunately, it was still a little depressing and cold. Maybe a Victorian kissing bough would help, I thought with a smile.

"Is there something amusing about our holiday decorations?"

Briggs asked.

"Amusing, no. Sad, yes. I was just making a mental note of how I might bring a bit of festive atmosphere to this place."

"It's a police station. I think plastic garland is about as festive as we can get. What brings you in here so late?"

"A horse and carriage," I answered. "And the Hawksworth murder case."

"Ah ha." He leaned his nicely chiseled forearms on the counter. "And how did you like the carriage ride?"

"Actually, I'm feeling just a tad angry at Henry Ford for that whole motor car idea. I think the entire world would be much more delightful if we all traveled in carriages." From my side, the counter was too tall to rest my forearms, so I curled my fingertips over the edge and leaned closer. We were face to face and just a few feet apart.

Under the ceiling lights, I saw that he had a tiny scar next to his eyebrow that I had never noticed before. Which was surprising because I had mentally catalogued just about every other attribute. "More delightful maybe but way less productive. And instead of streets being cluttered with cars they would be cluttered with . . . well, you know what happens around horses."

I laughed. "I hadn't thought about that. Anyhow, back to the Hawksworth murder. I went to the library as you suggested. I found an article about Hawksworth breaking ground on a big shipyard."

"Yes, that plan was squashed in the courts."

"I figured something stopped it since there is no shipyard down on the beach. But I noticed something very interesting. There was a picture of Bertram Hawksworth signing the documents for the contract. And he was holding one of those nib pens that they used back then."

"Why was that so interesting?"

"Because he was signing with his left hand."

He blinked at me, waiting for me to continue. But then his brows arched as if something had occurred to him. "The murder scene picture shows him holding the gun with his right hand," he said.

"Exactly."

"Hmm, interesting. You know there's a storage room where we keep boxes of evidence and reports from all the past cases. The earliest box is dated 1899 when the milkman got angry at a customer and threw a bottle of milk at his head. I know this because I was bored one day and I decided to open the box to see just what the police were dealing with back at the turn of the century. There's a box for the Hawksworth case. I hadn't mentioned it because, unlike all the other boxes, it is small and light. The case was closed so fast nothing much went inside of it."

I was practically on my tiptoes with interest as he went on about the box. Briggs was always good at reading my body language. He stopped his reasoning behind not bothering with the puny, near empty box and looked at me across the counter. "I take it you want to see the box."

"Yes," I said quickly. "If it's all right. My pets are waiting for me at home, so I won't be long."

"And you won't be long because, as I mentioned, the box is nearly empty. Don't get your hopes up too much." He buzzed me through to the official side of the counter and led me down a narrow hallway to a door. He unlocked the door and we headed down a set of metal stairs which ended at another door. Once again, he pulled out his keys to unlock the door.

"Jeez, this place feels like a prison," I quipped.

"Very funny." He opened the door and flicked on a light. The windowless basement room was filled with industrial shelving all piled high with boxes.

My gaze circled the room. "My gosh. Port Danby must have been like the wild west at some point in time. How can there be so many boxes?"

"Every crime, no matter how big or small, is stored inside this room. Not sure why, but I've been told by the higher ups to keep it all." Briggs headed to a corner shelf and pulled out a step stool. He climbed on top and reached up to the top shelf. He pulled out a box that was no bigger than a box for kid's sandals and stepped down.

I stared at the box, trying not to show my disappointment.

"Yep. Biggest crime in these parts for the past hundred plus years, and this is all we've got. No physical evidence at all. Not even the gun or the bullets." He walked it over to the table and opened the lid. Three pieces of paper were folded up and clipped together.

"That's rather odd, isn't it?" I asked. "To have no physical evidence inside."

He handed me the papers. "I've always thought so. It was almost as if the entire thing had been covered up or erased. Like someone was trying to squelch the story fast."

I unfolded the papers. The first one was a handwritten police report form filled out by an Officer Gaynor. I skimmed through his report. "He was the first officer on the scene." I ran my finger over the script and squinted to read it without my glasses and in the bad lighting. "Yuck. He goes into pretty graphic detail about the state of the bodies." I kept reading. "Those poor kids." I continued on to the second page and sucked in an excited breath. "Right here." I pointed to the second paragraph of the report which Officer Gaynor had written the day after the murder. "He noted the same thing." I read the lines to Briggs. "When looking through photographs of the Hawksworth family, I noticed that Bertram Hawksworth used his left hand to write." I looked up at Briggs. "He must have seen the same newspaper clipping as me. He goes on to note that the murder weapon was in his right hand when they found Hawksworth and his wife dead in the piano parlor."

Briggs pulled out the last sheet of paper and looked at it. "This is the report that claims it was a murder-suicide. It says on October 7th, 1906 at approximately six in the evening, Bertram Hawksworth shot his three children and his wife, Jill, before turning the pistol on himself. This report is signed by an Officer Turner. It's dated October 12th, 1906. He wrote *case closed* on the final line."

I took the paper from his hand. "But what happened to Officer Gaynor and the wrong hand theory?" I turned the papers over and looked once again into the empty box. There was nothing more to see.

I looked up at Briggs. "Seems as if we've just added another layer of mystery to the mystery."

# CHAPTER 7

*T*he buttery yellow facade coupled with the candy cane teal and white stripes on the window frames already made Elsie's Sugar and Spice Bakery look like an edible confection. But her incredible gingerbread display in the front window took it to an entirely new level. A whimsically shaped gingerbread house with candy stained glass windows, a peppermint striped chimney and thick white frosting icicles sat on a hill of snow that appeared to be made wholly of royal icing. Rows of swirly lollipops lined either side of a candy pebble walkway leading to the dark chocolate front door. Evergreen trees of piped green frosting and red cinnamon candies lined the entire scene, and strings of gingerbread people, each decorated to be unique, frolicked in the buttercream yard. A cake snowman was surrounded by a mound of fondant wrapped gift boxes, each one, like the gingerbread folk, was decorated with different colored ribbons and candy baubles.

I walked inside the bakery and had to set back the dial on my nose or get swept up into a dizzying sugar rush. Elsie's glass shelves were filled with dozens of amazing treats. I zeroed right in on a tray of almond horns. She had dipped each end in dark chocolate and she'd added red and green sprinkles for a festive touch.

I waited while Elsie finished with her customers.

"The town is already getting busy," Elsie said as she closed the register. "I saw you looking at the window display. What do you think?"

"I think I feel bad for poor Ryder, who arrived extra early this morning to work on the flower shop window. He might as well throw in the towel. Your display is magical, Elsie. Like you. I don't know how you do it."

She waved her hand as if it was no big deal to build an entire storybook scene out of cookie dough and sugar. And that was in between baking and running a store.

"It was a nice diversion." She released a slow breath. "But seeing how nice it's been for you to have Ryder in the shop, I'm thinking about taking on some help. Mind you, I've had assistants before, but they never worked out."

Lester, Elsie's twin brother and the coffee shop owner on the opposite side of me, had told me that no one was ever good enough for his sister. She was such a perfectionist and so big on control, she either scared off her new employees or they tossed their aprons on the counter and walked out in frustration. But I wanted to be supportive.

"You should advertise, Elsie. I know Ryder is an exception, and once he leaves, I'm sure I'll never find a suitable replacement. But I have to say, I love having him in the shop."

"You got lucky with that kid, that's for darn sure. And speaking of Ryder . . ." She lowered her voice as if the baked goods had ears. "Is it my imagination or does our mutual, boy crazy friend seem less interested in your amazing assistant than she did a few weeks ago? I don't see her finding excuses to walk across to your shop as much. And for awhile, she had replaced wearing some of those shabby rock and roll t-shirts with pretty winter sweaters. But she came in today wearing a Rolling Stones shirt and that faded brown fedora."

"Let's just say, there seems to be an indirect correlation between Lola's interest in a man and the man's interest in Lola."

Elsie looked puzzled by my math analogy.

"In other words, she stopped liking him once he liked her. I should get back over there. He's alone in the shop, and he's busy with the window. But I believe one of those almond horns is calling my name. I want this one from the front of the tray. It has the most chocolate. I'll take one for Ryder too."

Elsie slid open the door and plucked out the cookies. "Are we still on for making chocolate truffles tomorrow night?" she asked.

"Are you kidding? I've been having this recurring dream where I'm with Lucy and Ethel in the chocolate factory and I'm elbow deep in melted milk chocolate. We are definitely still on. I'm excited to learn the art of truffle making."

"Perfect. I will get everything ready."

I nibbled my almond horn and headed back to my shop with one for Ryder. Before I reached the door, I heard distinctly unhappy grumbling coming from Lester's side. I walked around to the Coffee Hutch. Since early fall when I moved into my shop, Lester and Elsie had been competing to have their sidewalk seating areas filled with customers. It didn't even matter if the people had spent money at their stores. Someone could easily have sat at one of Elsie's tables with a cup of Lester's coffee, and Les didn't mind if someone sat at his table with one of Elsie's cobblestone muffins. They just wanted their tables filled. I suppose it gave the look that business was thriving. Which it was for both of them, tables filled or not. That was when I, an only child, discovered that sibling rivalry stayed strong no matter how old you got. But the snowfall and glacial weather had dampened the competition some. It seemed even with Lester's plush seat cushions and Elsie's beautiful hand woven placemats, no one wanted to sit outside when the trees were dripping with icicles and the wind blowing in off the coast was bitterly cold.

Lester was attempting to get a very large wooden sleigh through the single door of the coffee shop.

"I'll hold the door, Les." I rushed over to help him.

"Oh thanks, Lacey. Didn't see you over there. Excuse my salty language."

"Didn't hear a thing. And I've been known to occasionally drop a salted word myself, so no worries."

He managed to get the sled into the shop, but it was so big, some of the indoor stools fell over. Lester placed the sleigh down hard on the ground. His face was red from struggling with the heavy sled and from the cold and mostly, it seemed, from anger. And Lester, with his snow white pillow of hair and colorful shirts and sweaters, rarely looked angry.

"Whose crazy idea was it to have this window display contest?" he grumbled. "I don't even know why I'm bothering. Did you see Elsie's window? It's ridiculous. Like she was asked to decorate a window for the White House."

"Ahh, now the sleigh and the salty language make sense. And, yes, I don't know why any of us bother with Elsie putting all her talents to use on her window." It hadn't even occurred to me that the window contest would be a new source of competition between Lester and Elsie. "Of course, I can't complain because Ryder is designing my window. Hey, why don't I help you put this into your window. Then we can figure out ways to spruce it up. I've got ribbons and holly leaves. I've even got some gold and silver garland in my shop."

Some of the red had cooled from his round cheeks. "You're a peach, Lacey. A pink peach."

"I'll be right back."

# CHAPTER 8

*A*fter an hour of helping Lester put together a window display and in between helping customers, I spent the rest of the morning creating a Victorian kissing bough. Thanks to Ryder's brilliantly crafted wire sphere it had turned out pretty. And I'd only suffered two hot glue gun burns in the process. I tied a frilly spray of mistletoe at the bottom with a bright blue strip of ribbon, and Ryder had fashioned a sturdy hook from wire for hanging.

It spun around as I held it up to admire. "What do you think?" I called to the front window.

Ryder leaned out. His jeans were covered with floral moss and white cedar bark chips. "It's awesome. You should make a few more if you have any holly leaves left."

I picked up the bag of holly. "I did go a little overboard with the pruning shears. I think I could make a couple more to sell and maybe one to hang in our shop."

"I'll build some more spheres."

"Only if you have time. How is it going? Do you need some help?"

"Nope. It's going just fine."

"I'm going to take this over to Lola's shop. I think it's the last part of her window display. Then we're going to grab some lunch at Franki's. Do you want something? Or maybe you'd like to crawl out of that window and go with us. We could close the shop for a bit."

Ryder crawled out from the bay window and sat on the edge of it. "I'll keep working. Besides, I think I annoy Lola."

"You don't. There's not one annoying bone in your body, Ryder. Lola is just kind of unpredictable with her moods." I didn't know how else to explain how she went from practically fawning over him one minute to hardly acknowledging his existence the next. "I could bring you a burger with fries," I suggested, wanting to take his mind off the Lola topic.

"Nah, don't worry about it. I'll get something later."

"If you're sure. Text if you change your mind."

I yanked the hood of my coat up over my head as I walked across the street to Lola's Antiques, the kissing bough swinging at my side. No new snow had fallen for several days, and rivulets of water flowed down Harbor Lane from the melt. I jumped over several puddles and a water filled gutter. At least the cold fog had burned off into a brisk blue day.

I stopped to admire Lola's front window. The girl had an eye for design. After her world traveling parents gave her permission to design the shop however she liked, Lola had transformed the exterior into a beautiful smoky gray-blue storefront with glistening picture windows and sheer curtains. It was a perfect blend of continental and small town.

I probably shouldn't have been too surprised about her incredible window display, except, so far, all she'd done was complain about having to drag old toys out from the storeroom. And drag she did. Sitting together in the window, the toys and antiques took you right back to a Victorian Christmas. The centerpiece and focal point of the display was an old fashioned bicycle with the massive front wheel and the teeny tiny rear wheel. Lola had woven some plaid ribbon through the wire thin spokes. A wooden rocking horse with a long flowing mane and tail sat next to a big silver metal goose pull toy. A charming antique sled that still had some of its original gold trim sat up against the window ledge, which was covered in fake snow. An ancient pair of ice skates rounded out the snow scene, and if that wasn't enough, Lola had filled the inside of an old Victorian dollhouse with the most intricately detailed miniature furniture I'd ever seen. There was so much to look at, I might have stood out there for another hour if Lola hadn't seen me gawking through the front window.

She opened the door. "Pink, what are you doing?" Her gaze dropped to the kissing bough dangling from my fingers. "Ahh! it's perfect," she said loudly enough to dislodge a mushy pile of snow from the roof top. It plopped down like melted ice cream between us. I stepped over it and followed Lola into the shop.

My nose went into instant twitching mode. "What is that pungent smell? Glue?"

"Yes, can you still smell it? I was gluing the handle on a vase, but it's too cold to open the window. The strong odor is making me a bit loopy."

"The last thing you need," I joked. "How did the vase break?"

Lola bowed with a flourish to point out her dog, Late Bloomer. The boxer lifted his graying muzzle from the pillow where he cradled a rawhide in his paws. His stubby tail swished back and forth when he realized he was the topic of our conversation.

"Bloomer just walked by and did that ear shake thing, and crash, the vase hit the ground. It's a valuable piece of Nippon. Or at least it was. Now it's a worthless vase held together with glue. I've always thought it was kind of ugly anyhow."

"So you rewarded Bloomer with a new rawhide?"

Lola laughed. "No. That he found in the farthest, deepest corner of the storeroom when I was pulling out the old toys. I think he dropped it there when he was a puppy, but it still looks new."

I patted Bloomer on the head. "It does look new. Ten thousand years from now people are going to dig in the ground and instead of finding fossils, they're going to find hidden rawhides all perfectly preserved."

"Man, they are going to think we were a bunch of weirdoes who gnawed on twisted leather for fun." Lola took the sphere from my hand. "You put a hook on it. Great. I've got a jutting nail in the small ceiling of the window." She held it up. "You are genius, my friend."

"I'd like to take the genius credit, but it was actually Ryder who created the form for the ball. All I did was cut holly and battle the hot glue gun."

"That was nice of him," she said quickly.

"Yes, don't forget to thank him when you see him."

"Uh huh," she said in a way that assured me she wouldn't. She climbed into the window and stepped gingerly around the fake snow. She hung the kissing bough up and jumped back down from the window. "I love it."

"You do realize that with the kissing bough hanging up there with your delicate display, there is no way anyone can use it to steal a kiss."

Lola rubbed her chin in thought. "I guess it does sort of defeat the purpose." She laughed. "Who am I kidding? No one worth kissing ever walks in here. Are we doing lunch at Franki's? I'm hungry."

"Yes, grab your coat. Let's go."

We stepped out onto the sidewalk and had to avoid the mosaic of puddles forming on the ground. "Did you take a carriage ride last night?" I asked her as we hurried across to Franki's.

"No. Just like hanging a kissing bough up in a window, a romantic carriage ride alone sort of defeats the purpose."

"I wasn't alone. I rode with Marty Tate. And he was far more charming than any man I've dated."

Lola had a good laugh at my comment as she pulled open the door.

Franki's Diner was crowded. People were beginning to arrive for the light show. And then, of course, there were the boat owners themselves. There were more than a few unfamiliar faces around the tables.

Lola and I sat at a table directly behind the stools running along the counter. They were filled too. Three men were sitting at the stools closest to our table. They had dropped a hat on one seat, apparently to save it. The hat was bright yellow and had the words Dayton Construction labeled across it. They looked as if they'd been out on a construction crew with steel toed boots and downy sleeveless vests. Lola zeroed right in on the many muscular arms but then her eyes were drawn to the front door. I was facing the back of the restaurant, but the sudden rush of cold air let me know someone had walked inside.

Lola was practically leaning into the aisle as she eyed the newest customer.

"Hey, Dayton, there you are." The man next to us picked up the yellow hat. He pointed down at Dayton's wet work boots. "What happened? Did you step in a puddle? I told you to put the waterproof stuff on them." The guy giving the lecture stuck out his heavy work boot and turned it as if he was admiring a fine pair of shoes at a shoe shop. "Mine are dry as the desert."

Dayton ignored the man's advice. Lola had caught his eye. He turned to flash her a gracious smile before climbing up on the stool between his friends. He was tall, lean and thirty something with mint green eyes that could be considered very attractive. He had an impressive head of blond wavy hair beneath the yellow cap. But, in my opinion, the sharp angles of his face, his wide jaw and straight mouth, made him look sort of mean. It seemed my friend did not share that opinion. Lola's smile lingered long after he climbed onto his stool and faced away from us.

Franki arrived at our table. "It's a madhouse in here today. What do you two girls want?" She pulled out her order pad.

"I'll have the turkey on wheat." I folded the menu.

Franki and I looked over at Lola who was still admiring the construction worker from behind.

I kicked her foot under the table to get her attention. As she turned to me, Franki's phone rang. "Just a second, Lola," Franki said as she pulled out her phone. She rolled her eyes, which meant it was probably one of her four kids.

Lola kicked my foot back and motioned with her head toward the man on the stool. "What is it about men in steel toed boots?" she sighed and then leaned closer. "He is so incredible. I wonder where he's from."

"From a construction site, I imagine."

Franki stopped her phone conversation for a second to fill us in. "I think they are building a mansion over on Beacon Cliffs. They must have gotten tired of that grease pit of a diner in Chesterton." She went right back to her conversation. And from the tidbits I heard, it seemed Tyler might have injured himself at basketball practice.

"It's in the medicine cabinet, behind the gauze," Franki said with exasperation. "Did you ice it? Good. I'll take a look at it when I get home." She hung up and grunted as she tucked the phone back into her apron. "Tyler pulled a muscle in his leg at basketball practice. Now he's going to smell like spearmint. I don't know why that healing ointment has to be so pungent. Taylor did the same thing last month, and the girls refused to let him sit at the dinner table. Which was fine with him because that meant he got to eat on the couch in front of the television." She looked at Lola. "Aside from that tall house builder behind me, Lola, what would you like?"

Lola pretended to be shocked but then laughed. "Was I being that obvious?"

"Yes," Franki and I said simultaneously.

"I'll have chicken soup and corn bread." Lola said as she folded the menu.

"And pie," a deep voice added behind Franki.

Dayton was turned on the stool and smiling at Lola. There was something about his smile that didn't seem genuine. "If the lady doesn't mind sticking around to share a piece with me after lunch."

Lola practically melted into a pool of butter right there on the vinyl seat. "I don't mind."

He nodded politely at all of us and turned back to eat with his friends.

Lola fanned her face. "It sure is warm in here today."

"Isn't it though?" Franki said as she collected the menus and walked away.

# CHAPTER 9

$\mathcal{L}$ ola had impatiently tapped the table with her fingers and the floor with her foot, waiting for me to eat my sandwich. I decided to have Franki wrap half of it to go so I wouldn't choke to death trying to inhale it. Lola didn't touch her soup and only picked at the cornbread. Her excitement about having a slice of pie with the tall stranger made me a bit nervous. She was just a little too anxious.

Since my lunch had been cut short, I decided to finish the second half of my sandwich during a walk on the beach. On any other given day, in the winter, Pickford Beach would've been close to deserted. Today, it was more crowded on the sand than the pier because people were milling about the beach watching the boats get decked out with holiday lights. For the second time, I caught Detective Briggs standing on the sand watching the activities out on the water.

He was so focused on the boats, he didn't hear me walk up.

"I think I've discovered something new about my friend Detective Briggs," I said as I reached him.

Briggs turned around. "Miss Pinkerton." He said my name in such a way that made me think, *he enjoys running into me as much as I enjoy running into him*. Of course, it might have just been wishful thinking on my part. "What have you discovered about me?"

"You like boats. Or maybe you like holiday decorations. But judging by the decor in the police station, I'm going to stick with my first theory."

He had been leaving his beard stubble even heavier in the winter weather, but it never detracted from his appealing grin, which was sort of lopsided. But in a good way. "You're right. I do like boats. Especially nice sailing sloops like that one, *Cloud Nine* with the T. Ruxley Plumbing sign."

"Now T. is the brother of the other Ruxley?"

"Yes."

"I could see you at the helm in a jaunty captain's hat and possibly a white polo shirt."

He shook his head. "No polo shirt. But I'd take the captain's hat. Unfortunately, my job doesn't allow me time or extra income for a sailboat."

"Never give up on your dreams, Detective Briggs."

He smiled at me. "I'll try not to, Miss Pinkerton. Oh, by the way, I found out something interesting about Officer Gaynor, the man who filled out the original report on the Hawksworth murder."

"You did?"

"Yes, I did. Along with those dusty old boxes, there is a giant file cabinet that contains folders for each of the employees of the police department. I did some digging and found out Officer Gaynor was taken off the case and transferred to the Mayfield station two days after he wrote the original report."

A group of high school kids came bounding across the sand. We stepped out of their way or risked getting run down by chattering, laughing teens.

"This event sure has everyone's adrenaline pumping," Briggs noted. "Which almost always leads to trouble of some kind."

"That sounds rather ominous coming from the head of the police department."

His thick, dark lashes dropped in a touch of embarrassment.

"Sorry, that was one of those thoughts better left in my head. It's just Port Danby is usually such a sleepy little town in winter, but events like this always stir up a lot of dust." More kids stomped by as he finished, spraying our shoes with wet sand.

"And sand apparently." I shook off my ankle boot. "Back to Officer Gaynor—did it say why he was transferred?"

"That's the interesting part. No reason was given, and there are even lines on the form to explain the transfer. They were blank."

We walked closer to the pier where it was quieter. I ducked to avoid a seagull that had braved the mob of people on the beach to pick up a crumb of food. "It almost sounds as if someone wanted Officer Gaynor off the case. Off the Port Danby police force even."

"That is one theory. I don't know much about how things were run back then, but it would have taken someone with considerable power to do that. And then there's the much less nefarious reason that they were shorthanded in Mayfield and they needed Officer Gaynor. Since the report is incomplete, we won't ever know for sure."

Briggs motioned toward the pier. "I'm heading back to the office. Are you going that way too?"

I pulled my sandwich out of my pocket. "I came down here to eat the rest of my lunch before heading back to work."

He nodded. "Just watch out for hungry seagulls and exuberant teenagers."

"I will. It seems the mystery deepens on the Hawksworth case. Thank you for looking into that, by the way. I know you're terribly busy, Detective Briggs."

"I wasn't all that busy." He glanced behind him to the pier where two teenage boys were throwing slushy snowballs at each other. Naturally, one of the wet balls of ice hit an innocent bystander, who didn't look too pleased. "But I think I will be soon enough."

# CHAPTER 10

*I* nibbled my sandwich and watched as the anchored boats danced in the choppy water, their bows dipping and rising with the current. Most of the boat owners had small inflatable dinghies and row boats in the water to get back and forth to shore and travel between other boats. Long strands of lights dangled from tall masts and sails. In daylight, they looked like tangled messes of wires and cords. I was sure they would be spectacular at night. Some of the boat owners had gone slightly overboard with decorations, filling their decks with mechanical Santas and reindeer, inflatable snowmen and garlands that nearly weighed down the hulls. Other boats went less for quantity and more for quality, or, at the very least, organized chaos. I had never seen a flotilla of holiday lights, and I was looking forward to it.

Most of the spectators were standing higher up on the sand, away from the perpetual mist the ocean provided. I decided to endure the salty spray instead of the crowd. My naturally curly hair had already curled into a Shirley Temple mop-like mound. I'd discovered mere weeks after moving to Port Danby that my flat iron was useless in coastal weather. After fighting the natural curl in my hair for years with every weapon known to woman, I waved the white flag of surrender and shoved my collection of flat irons and other hair torture devices into the bottom drawer of my dresser. I'd found a certain degree of relief in my new found freedom. My hair seemed happier too.

Even through the thick briny air and with the flurry of food smells coming off the pier, my sandwich enjoyment was interrupted by a strong, pungent odor. I twitched my nose from side to side to catch the direction of the toxic smell. I swept my gaze along the boats and zeroed in on my target. The odor was coming from *Cloud Nine*, the boat Detective Briggs had been admiring from the beach. A tall, broad shouldered man with a red Santa hat pulled down over his dark hair was painting a coat of varnish on a large wooden cutout of a nutcracker that looked as if it had seen better days. Apparently, the coat of toxic smelling glaze was his last effort to save the fading paint on his custom holiday decoration. Interestingly enough, he was so busy with his task, he hadn't noticed the man climbing up from a row boat onto the stern of *Cloud Nine*. I recognized the row boat man with impressive gray sideburns as Chad Ruxley, the man Briggs had spoken to briefly the day before. I could only assume the man with the paintbrush was T. Ruxley, Chad's estranged brother.

Footsteps finally alerted T. Ruxley that he had a visitor. He turned around and I got an amusing view of the felt reindeer sewn on the front of his sweater. It was a humorous ensemble that definitely didn't match the anger on his face when he saw Chad Ruxley walking across the deck. They faced each other without stepping into one another's personal space. There was nothing warm or spirited or brotherly about their greeting. While their physiques were quite different, they both had similarly shaped noses and chins.

I tried to filter out some of the extraneous noise around me to hear what they were arguing about, but by the time their words finished the long, choppy journey to shore, they sounded like sharp, angry pangs of noise.

Nosy posy that I was, I watched them argue for a few more minutes. T. Ruxley had taken the defensive body position and crossed his arms. Chad, on the other hand, was using a lot of hand motions and wild arm movements to get his point across. Whatever that point was. The shouting match ended with both men wearing angry scowls, but no punch had been thrown.

Chad threw his leg over the railing and climbed down a rope ladder to the small boat below. Water curled up over the lip of the row boat as he sat down hard. He grabbed the oars and sliced them into the water as he headed back toward his own boat. I looked back up at the deck of T. Ruxley's boat. Ruxley had yanked off the Santa hat. He clutched it in his hand as he glowered over the railing and watched his brother row away.

I'd procrastinated long enough with my turkey sandwich. I made my way back up the pier and along the wharf. A circle of people had gathered on the corner of Pickford Way and Harbor Lane. I hurried my pace to see what had caught their attention, but I figured it out long before I reached the circle of onlookers. A rousing rendition of Deck the Halls drowned out all the other noise on the street. I reached the spectators and peered through to the performers.

The professional caroling group consisted of three women and two men. The women were clad in richly colored bell-shaped skirts that moved stiffly as if supported by authentic crinoline underskirts. The layered flounces of one skirt stood out in a cerulean blue and red plaid. One singer with pretty red hair and round cheeks exposed white puffy pantalets as she crooned out her fa la las. Her fur trimmed mantelet was a rich cherry red. It went smartly with the black fur muff, which warmed both her hands, and, conveniently enough, held her song book. Her bonnet was trimmed in a green and red tartan ribbon that I quickly decided would look great around a holiday bouquet.

The men were dressed in cutaway tail coats and brightly colored trousers. Black top hats and shiny leather spats finished off the look. It seemed they took their costuming very seriously. They sang wonderfully too. Yolanda had outdone herself once again. I was looking forward to the evening's festivities.

# CHAPTER 11

*I* figured my pets would give me the evil eye for leaving the house again in the evening so I lured them into blissful delirium with their favorite treats. Nevermore was cleaning the tuna juice off his whiskers with his paws, taking the time to lick each foot for every drop of fish flavored syrup, as I pulled on my coat. Kingston hadn't once looked up from his feast of hardboiled eggs as I tossed my scarf around my neck. For my last bit of swaddling, I yanked on a red striped beanie to keep my head warm and keep my hair from doing the Medusa snake thing with curls lunging out in every direction.

Parking near the wharf was limited so Lola, Elsie, Les and I had made plans to walk to the marina. My house was at the top of the hill, so it made sense for me to walk down to Elsie's house, where she and Lester would be waiting. Lola lived farther down past Graystone Church, so she decided to wait at the antique shop for us to swing by and pick her up. I hadn't spoken to her since her impromptu pie date, but she'd texted that she had lots to talk about.

With my pets now tipsy from the treats, I slipped out easily. I locked the door and bounded down the front steps. Music and a rainbow-colored glow filled the night sky over Pickford Beach. Even my favorite site, the Pickford Lighthouse, twinkled with holiday spirit.

The night could have easily been ruined by heavy fog, a common occurrence in the winter months, but it was crystal clear all the way down to the water.

"Hey, *there's* Waldo," Dash called cheerily from his front porch.

I spun around to look at him. He was pointing up to his head, which was covered with a black cowboy hat. (As if the man needed anything to make him look more breathtaking.) "The red and white striped beanie," he said as he trotted down his porch steps. "It reminds me of that *Where's Waldo* book."

I patted my beanie. "And yet I'm sure I won't get lost in a crowd wearing this."

He reached up and pulled one curl before letting it spring back to its permanent coil. I hadn't expected the slightly intimate gesture and wasn't sure how to react. But before I could figure out my feelings about it, he spoke again.

"Are you walking down to the light show?" he asked. "Do you mind if I walk with you?"

I was still recovering from the hair touch, and it took me a second to answer. He mistook my hesitation as me not wanting to walk with him. I couldn't see his eyes well under the shadow of his hat brim, but his mouth turned down on the sides. "That's all right. I'm sure you have other people to walk with."

"No. I mean, yes, I'm going with Elsie and Lester and eventually Lola, but of course you can walk with us. The more the merrier, right?"

He didn't look convinced.

"Really, Dash. I welcome the company down the hill."

"If you're sure."

"Absolutely."

We made our way down Myrtle Place. Most everyone in the adjacent neighborhoods had already gone down to the marina to grab the best viewing spots.

"I was on the beach today watching the boats get ready, but I didn't see you. Did Yolanda finally set you free of light hanging duty?"

Dash adjusted his hat down so the uphill breeze wouldn't kick it off. He did it with the same cool finesse as a real cowboy. "Yes, thank goodness. That woman wears me out. I went to Beacon Cliffs this morning for a job interview. I need some work while the boat repair business is in a lull."

I looked over at him. "Job interview? At Beacon Cliffs? Don't tell me you were interviewing to work as a butler or chauffeur in one of those big fancy houses."

"Couldn't you just see me in a tuxedo carrying a tray of brandy glasses? I interviewed for a job on a construction site. They are building one of those *big fancy* houses, and they need more men."

"Dayton Construction?" I asked.

"Yeah, that's it. How'd you know?"

I attempted a shrug but realized I was too bundled in winter layers to pull it off. "I saw them at Franki's Diner this afternoon. When do you start?"

"I could start there tomorrow, but I called and told them I had another offer."

We turned the corner on Elsie's street. "You're popular. What was the other offer?"

He moved his mouth side to side and adjusted his hat again. It seemed he didn't want to answer. "Cleaning Mayor Price's chimney," he muttered.

"That doesn't seem like a job that will get you through the dry spell."

He cleared his throat. "It's a day at the most. I don't know why I didn't take the job, and I'm not lazy," he added quickly and unnecessarily.

"Uh, take it from the neighbor who hears you drilling, hammering and sawing long after the work day, I know you're not lazy."

"Sorry about that." We reached Elsie's walkway. Dash turned to me. "The truth is, after I left the interview I decided I didn't want to work for the owner, Randall Dayton. There was just something about him that made me think *stay clear*. You don't want to work for that guy."

Before I could get further details, Elsie's front door flew open. Surprisingly, Lola was the first person out the door. Elsie and Lester followed. The winter weather had forced Lester to temporarily pack away his brightly colored Hawaiian shirts. I was still getting used to seeing him bundled in winter wear. I missed the Hawaiian shirts, but Lester's smile always reminded me of sunshine.

"Hello, Dash," Lola said cheerily and then wrapped her arm around mine.

"Hey, Lola," Dash replied and hung back to join Lester and Elsie on the sidewalk.

Lola and I led the way. "I thought we were picking you up at the antique shop."

"I was bored so I drove up here." Lola squeezed my arm. I could tell she was extremely excited about something. After my brief, cryptic conversation with Dash, I was keeping my gloved fingers crossed that it didn't have anything to do with Randall Dayton.

"Forgive me for noticing, my dear friend, but you are positively giddy. Is it just the anticipation of the light show?" I asked, with a hopeful tone.

"The light show?" She laughed. "Please, I've seen it a dozen times. I swear some of the boat owners never even replace or update their decorations. No, I'm excited because I'm going on a carriage ride tonight."

"Are you? It is fun. Can I join you?"

She laughed again. "I'd love to have you along, but I think you might be a third wheel. I'm going with Randall Dayton, or as you probably know him, pie man."

She was so thrilled about it, I didn't want to show one ounce of worry or angst about the prospect. And besides, Dash really didn't have any concrete reason not to like the guy. It seemed he just didn't want to work for him.

"That's wonderful, Lola. It sounds very romantic."

"I thought so too." She hugged my arm tighter and practically made me skip through town just to keep up with her stride.

With any luck, Randall Dayton would show big interest in my best friend, and she would drop him like a lump of hot coal.

# CHAPTER 12

*R*yder poked his head out from the bay window as I walked into the shop. "How was the light show last night?"

"So you weren't there. I was looking around for you." I approached the window cautiously. He didn't tell me to stop. He'd covered the front panes with paper so no one passing by could see his work in progress. He'd asked me to stay clear too.

"Can I take a peek?" I asked.

"I guess."

He leaned out of the way as I looked into the window space. With wire and chicken coop fencing, white birch chips and white rose petals, Ryder had created an adorable three foot high polar bear who was sitting back in a snow drift made purely of white carnations. Two jolly sunflower seed penguins were halfway on their way to playing and tummy sliding through the carnation snow.

"Ryder—" I was nearly speechless. "You are so talented. I love it."

A wide smile crossed his face. "I wasn't too sure at first, but I think the bear turned out pretty cool."

"Are you kidding? I wish he wasn't made of perishable material. I'd keep him in that window all year." I pulled my eyes from the playful scene. "How did you get all this done?"

"My friends couldn't make it to the light show, which was fine. I've seen it so often. Some of the decorations are getting kind of tired and old. I decided to work on the window instead."

I smiled thinking about what Lola had said about the overused decorations. They had so much in common. "I feel guilty that you worked so late."

"Nah, I'm enjoying this. How was the flotilla?"

I tilted my head side to side to show I was slightly underwhelmed. "It was all right. I mean, don't get me wrong, it was spectacular to see all those sparkling lights against the backdrop of the black night sky. It reminded me of that Lite Bright toy I had as a kid. But there were so many people. It was just a touch too hectic for me."

"I could hear the noise all the way up here. Were you with Lola?" he asked unexpectedly.

"Uh, yes. I was. Elsie, Les, Dash, Lola and I walked down together." I certainly didn't need to mention that Lola left early for her date. "Which reminds me, I had several people ask me to make them a kissing bough. People have been admiring the one hanging in Lola's shop window. I hate to pull you from this monumental task, but if you could . . ."

Ryder pointed past me to my work island. "Already made four more spheres for you."

I sighed. "When you leave me to travel the arboretums and rain forests of the world, I'm just going to retire."

Even his deep laugh was likable. He turned back to the window display, and I headed to my office. As I passed the front door, I spotted Lola crossing the street looking like the cat who caught the mouse. I couldn't let her come inside and gush about her carriage ride. Ryder would overhear.

"I'll be right back, Ryder," I called and hurried out to meet her.

I could see the dreamy stars in Lola's brown eyes long before she reached the curb. "I was just coming to see you," she said. "Are you going somewhere?"

I badly wanted to let her know that I'd stepped out to spare Ryder the displeasure of hearing her gush about her date, but I kept quiet.

I motioned toward the Coffee Hutch. "I was going to go buy a hot cocoa. Since it seems you're bursting to tell me, how did things go last night?" I hadn't gotten much more out of Dash last night except that he just *didn't get good vibes* from Randall Dayton. That very general assessment wasn't enough to mention to Lola or ruin her newfound elation.

Lola hugged herself, and I was sure it didn't have to do with the chill in the air. "It was magical. We took a double ride and then we walked along the pier. We talked and laughed. Then we went into Franki's about midnight and shared a plate of pancakes. I wanted to pinch myself. And he's so handsome. Only one complaint. I think he smokes. I smelled tobacco on his clothes."

"Yuck. That's too bad." I was sure that dirty little fact would put a quick end to the budding romance. Like me, Lola had a huge distaste for cigarette smoking. I could usually detect a smoker from fifty feet away just by the smell on their clothes. "I didn't notice him smelling like tobacco when he walked into the diner. Maybe there were just too many other scents floating around. "

"I sat across from him and ate pie, and I didn't notice a thing. Even though I don't have a sensitive nose like you, I can always smell it on people. Like I did last night when I met Randall at the carriage stop. It was instant."

As we spoke, a siren sounded in the distance. It was a clear day so sound traveled far.

"I guess that sort of puts a quick end to it then," I said.

Lola's brows pushed up the edge of her beanie. "End to what?"

"The new romance?"

She gave a half-hearted shrug. She was obviously torn. "I could probably look past it as long as he doesn't light one up around me."

"I see." I tried not to sound judgy, but Lola knew I was being exactly that.

"We don't all have the two most eligible men in town vying for our attention, Pink. I can't be that picky. There just aren't that many totally perfect men in the world."

I looked pointedly back to my bay window, where, behind the

strips of brown packing paper, a perfectly perfect guy who liked Lola was toiling away on my window display. "Right. And by the way, I don't have anyone vying for my attention."

"Right," she repeated curtly.

The sirens grew louder. There was more than one now. It seemed that people were migrating toward the wharf. I was glad for the diversion from our conversation. "I wonder what's going on?"

Lola and I both walked toward the street to get a better view of the beach. Red flashing lights and screaming sirens startled us as they raced past on Harbor Lane.

"Something has happened down at the marina." I hurried to the flower shop and poked my head inside.

Ryder was out of the window. "I just saw emergency vehicles. What's happening out there?"

"Not sure. I'm going to head down to the marina and find out. I'll be right back." Lola had gone back to her shop. I knew she wasn't terribly pleased with me after our chat. I hadn't meant to crush her romantic dreams. I'd apologize later. After I found out just what the heck was going on down by the water.

I wasn't the only curious person rushing along the sidewalk to Pickford Marina. I noticed that Detective Briggs' car had moved from in front of the station to a block away at the entrance to the pier. His assistant, Officer Chinmoor, was trying his hardest to keep onlookers from swarming the pier and, more specifically, the fish cleaning station. That seemed to be where the activity was happening.

Like a salmon swimming upstream, I hurried past the people being directed off the pier. I spotted Detective Briggs with his notebook looking at something behind the brick retaining wall where fishermen stopped to clean their catch. It was a favorite hangout for pelicans, seagulls and other seafaring birds, but there were no hungry birds hovering overhead today. The human ruckus below had scared them off.

I headed toward Detective Briggs. Officer Chinmoor's long thin arm stretched out to stop me.

"Sorry, Miss Pinkerton, I can't let you through. This is a crime scene."

Detective Briggs heard him mention my name. He glanced back over his shoulder. "It's all right, Officer Chinmoor, you can let her through." My heart did a little skippity skip, but I had to quickly tamp that down. From the solemn looks on the faces around me, it seemed I was about to see something grim and a skipping heart just wasn't appropriate.

I reached Detective Briggs' side and stepped around to the back of the wall. Chad Ruxley was curled on his side between a pile of discarded fishing nets and two broken pallets. And from the pallor of his skin, my brief medical training assured me he was dead.

# CHAPTER 13

*C*had Ruxley, the stout, forty something owner of Ruxley Plumbing and the owner of the twenty foot sailing sloop *Sea Gem* looked peaceful, almost as if he'd decided to just curl up for a nap amongst the worn out fishing nets. He had on a bright blue sweater and a khaki colored winter coat, and his hands were covered with black gloves. But his face was a ghastly gray, and his lips and finger-tips were as white as the piles of snow around him. In a macabre twist, a festive piece of tartan ribbon was jammed between his chin and his chest.

Nate Blankenship, the local coroner, was already at the scene. He was crouched near the body checking for rigor mortis and body temperature. A dead body slowly loses its biological warmth and reaches ambient temperature or the temperature of its surroundings.

The coroner stood. "The temperature is just above freezing out on this wharf, which makes things a little harder to calculate because it slows down rigor mortis, but I'd say this man died at about eleven o'clock last night."

Briggs added that to his list of notes. "That makes sense. The crowds would have cleared out by then. I wasn't here last night, but Hilda said the light show and festivities ended around ten."

"James, (The coroner and Briggs were on a first name basis. Lucky Nate.) did you notice the lump on the back of his head?"

Briggs put his notebook in his pocket and walked around to where the coroner was kneeling. He crouched down with a gloved hand and felt the spot on the back of Ruxley's skull. "That's why you're the doctor, and I just piece together the evidence," Briggs said to Nate.

Nate pulled back Ruxley's collar to expose a grisly cut and bruising on his neck. "The marks on his neck are obvious and consistent with this piece of ribbon. It's the kind my wife uses to make holiday bows for the tree. It has wire running along each side to make it easy to shape."

They stood up and pondered the position of the body. I couldn't stop myself from interjecting. "It certainly doesn't look as if he struggled at all. It almost looks as if he just curled up here by the nets to nap. Maybe he was knocked unconscious first and then strangled."

Nate Blankenship had only met me briefly at a murder scene in Mayfield when a popular food blogger was killed with her favorite coffee creamer. He knew I'd had a hand in solving that crime with my super sense of smell, so rather than look askance at my help, he seemed to welcome it. Especially after Briggs told him I had also spent several years in medical school.

Nate nodded approvingly at my assessment. "Since he didn't struggle or fight someone off, I probably won't find any skin or DNA under the victim's fingernails." He elbowed Briggs. "Which makes your job that much harder."

"Detective Briggs." Officer Chinmoor came up behind us. He was fidgeting with his gun belt, something he did when he was nervous. "We've got Timothy Ruxley here now. I haven't told him the news yet. There were no other people on the victim's boat. He appeared to be alone."

Briggs sighed. "Another part of the job that's hard. If you'll excuse me, Nate. The victim's brother was out here on one of the other boats. I need to break the news to him. I'll ask him if he wants to identify him right now or wait until he's taken to the morgue. Sometimes that is less shocking."

Detective Briggs walked around us and out to the pier where Tim Ruxley stood, looking rather pale and rubbing his arms and shoulders for warmth. White, hazy breaths puffed from his mouth as he nervously eyed the emergency vehicles and personnel around the wharf.

"The air is especially frigid this morning so scent molecules will be scarce," Nate noted, bringing my attention back to the murder scene. "But maybe you'd like to take your nose for a spin around the victim's clothing and hair. There might be some invisible evidence that needs sniffing out."

"Of course. And yes, I agree the weather is going to make it a difficult task." I crouched down next to the body and hovered my face over him. It was always an eerie feeling to get so close to a dead person, as if at any second they might pop open their eyes and yell surprise and send me straight into orbit. But Chad Ruxley wasn't going anywhere, and from the terrible bruising on his neck and the shade of blue around his mouth, I was certain he wouldn't be yelling surprise again . . . ever.

The glacial air and the strong fish odor wafting off the nets masked any scents on Ruxley's clothing. It seemed he ate something with onions the night before, possibly a burger or steak. As I pushed my face closer and drew my nose along his coat, I noticed a small rip in the fabric just below the coat pocket. A section of the khaki material was gone. I moved back toward his neck and ran my nose closer to the ribbon, the decorative murder weapon. Two smells mingled together around the ribbon and the collar of his sweater, making it hard to distinguish one from the other. One reminded me of the glue Lola was using to fix the vase and the other was sweeter, like the smell of wood. I made a mental note of what I thought they might be and finished my nasal inspection. Other than the unexpected odors around the ribbon and the sweater, there was nothing to report.

As I stood, I saw that Detective Briggs was leading Timothy Ruxley to the body. The man didn't look nearly as distraught as I'd expected. But then they had parted ways. And that thought reminded me of what I'd witnessed as I ate my turkey sandwich on the beach.

I waited quietly off to the side as Tim Ruxley gave a positive iden- tification of the murder victim. "Yes that's Chad," he said quietly. For a second I thought I detected a waver in his voice. But it might have been my imagination.

Detective Briggs took a few contact details down from the victim's brother before walking over to talk to me. "Miss Pinkerton, were you able to detect anything of note on the victim?"

I hesitated, not sure if I had anything solid enough to share, but I forged ahead. "First, something I noticed that you might have already seen. There is a tear in the shell of his coat, and it seems a piece of fabric is missing."

He tapped his notepad. "Yes, I made note of that. Anything else?" I was thrilled to have him value and trust my smell skills so much. But I was disappointed that I didn't have anything concrete.

"When I was smelling the ribbon and the collar of his sweater, two things drifted out to Philomena." I pointed to my nose.

He responded with a questioning brow lift.

"You're right. Now that I hear it out loud, it doesn't work at all. Anyhow, back to the smells. They were sort of dancing around each other, so it was hard to pinpoint either one. And then there are the terribly foul smelling fish nets. And, of course, Philo—my nose doesn't work as well when it's cold outside, but I smelled a fresh woodsy fragrance. And in between little sparks of the woodsy fragrance, I caught whiffs of something chemical. Some kind of solvent or glue or possibly a paint thinner of some kind. I'm sorry I can't be more specific. The traces of scent are miniscule and circumstances are making it too difficult to get a solid smell."

Briggs pulled out his notepad and wrote down my rather rambling, disjointed description.

"I'm sorry I can't be more definitive," I said.

"Not at all. Each of the those smells falls into a pretty specific cate- gory of odors. They might just help." He glanced back to see that Tim Ruxley was gone. "Frankly, the brother's reaction was fairly under- whelming. Even if they were estranged, it would be shocking to hear that your brother had been murdered. And during a holiday festival event. I think we'll be starting with him as a possible person of interest."

I nodded quickly. "And, on that account, I can give you something much more concrete. Yesterday, after you left the pier, I walked down to the water to eat the rest of my turkey sandwich. Something caught my attention out near the boats—" I stopped and drew in an excited breath. "Oh my gosh, I just remembered what it was that caught my attention. It was the pungent smell of varnish." I had to slow down so Briggs could keep up with his pen. "Timothy Ruxley was painting varnish over the hand painted nutcracker standing at the railing of his boat. The boat you were admiring yesterday, the *Cloud Nine*."

Briggs looked up when things clicked in his mind. "Varnish? Do you think that's the smell on his clothes?"

I scrunched my nose. It was really hampered by the cold. "I'm not sure, but it could be. But that's not all. While he was painting the nutcracker, his brother"—I nodded respectfully toward the body —"rowed up to the *Cloud Nine*. He climbed on board. Uninvited, I could only assume, due to the cold greeting he got from Timothy. They argued loudly for a few minutes and then Chad climbed back down to his boat and rowed away."

"Did you catch what the argument was about?"

"I couldn't make out the words, but the body language and the angry faces assured me it was an argument."

Briggs put away his notes. "We're going to finish up here, Miss Pinkerton. You've been a great help this morning. I hate to take up any more of your time, but—"

"Yes," I said with way too much zeal.

He released a quiet laugh. "I guess you've anticipated what I'm about to ask you."

I tapped my head. "Like our minds are synced up. You want me to go on board the *Cloud Nine* with you and sniff around for the matching smell on Ruxley's clothes."

He smiled. "I guess we do think in unison."

"Like two choreographed detective brains."

"I can't search the boat without a warrant. And even then, this is a unique predicament. I'm pretty fuzzy on maritime law and bound-aries, but I'd probably need to get the coast guard involved. Still, I thought you could twitch that little button nose around and see if anything is amiss."

"My button nose and I are at your service. Just text me and I'll come by the station when you're ready to go out to the boat."

"Great. Thanks."

"No, Detective Briggs, thank you. I'm in need of a good mystery to solve." I looked politely toward the victim. "No disrespect to you, Mr. Ruxley, of course."

"I'll see you later then, Miss Pinkerton."

"Yes you will, Detective Briggs."

# CHAPTER 14

$\mathcal{I}$ held up my newly finished kissing bough to admire and decided it needed a colorful bow on top. The bough had turned out so nicely, I decided to hang it in my shop. Ryder had already volunteered to climb the step ladder and add a hook to the ceiling.

I checked my phone for the hundredth time to see if Detective Briggs had texted. I chastised myself for being so excited about a new murder case. But I just couldn't slow the rush of adrenaline. And it didn't hurt that I'd be working alongside my favorite detective either. When we weren't working on a case together, we were both so busy with our jobs and other aspects of our lives, we rarely spoke or saw each other. It was sort of depressing to think that a murder had to happen for the two of us to hang out together. But I'd accepted it as a fact of life. And now, someone had died by nefarious means, which was terrible and tragic, of course, but it also meant I would get to solve a case with Briggs. Or at least try to solve it. The last two cases had been successful, but there was never any guarantee that a case would come to a conclusive end. Much like the Hawksworth murders. I was sure that if that poor family had been murdered in this century, the sketchy evidence wouldn't have been so quickly considered concrete and the true perpetrator would have been found. And I was certain that the murderer was not the left-handed Mr. Hawksworth.

I stood in front of the wall space where all my ribbon spools hung in a rainbow colored waterfall. I tapped my chin as I glanced from the bough to the wall of ribbon. "Blue and silver," I said, confidently.

"What's that?" Ryder asked. He was at the potter's bench on the other side of the store arranging some floral bouquets in silver and gold vases.

"Oh, nothing. I was just thinking aloud about ribbon choice." I pulled out a strand of blue and a strand of silver ribbon from their respective spools. I snipped them off and held them up. "What do you think of this color combo for our kissing bough?"

"I like it. Reminds me of winter."

"That's what I think too." I turned to my work island and tied the ribbons around the top wire of the bough. As I worked, my mind drifted to the murder scene and more specifically the murder ribbon. I'd seen a similar ribbon or possibly even one just like it adorning the carolers' bonnets.

Something big clicked in my mind, and I nearly rolled the kissing bough off the counter. One of the caroler's was named Ruxley. Was it just a coincidence? The woman's name was Charlene. I'd have to let Detective Briggs know immediately. And then, as if Briggs had been reading my mind, the phone rang.

"Hello."

"Miss Pinkerton, I've arranged for Tim Ruxley to ferry us out to his boat on his inflatable dinghy. Is this a good time for you?"

"Absolutely. I'll get my coat and scarf and head right over. And, Detective Briggs, I forgot to mention, one of the carolers has the last name Ruxley."

"Yes, I know. You already gave me that clue before the actual crime."

I fell quiet as I tried to go back through the dozens of conversations I'd had with people in the past few days. It dawned on me just as he reminded me.

"On Wednesday, we ran into each other and you were surprised to hear me say Ruxley because you had seen it on the carolers' list."

"Yes, that's right. I don't know why it didn't occur to me this morning."

"I spoke to Tim Ruxley about it. He seemed to be dodging the question some but then admitted that Charlene Ruxley was Chad Ruxley's ex-wife. Tim insisted he wanted to be the one to tell her about the murder. He is expecting my visit though. I've assured him it's just to get some further information. I'll wait for you here at the station. Then we can head out on our sea adventure."

"I'm on my way."

I didn't actually run to the police station, but I walked the two blocks at a very good clip. Detective Briggs stepped out as I reached the door.

"That was fast," he said. "I'll fill you in some on the way to the beach. Tim Ruxley has offered to wait on shore with his inflatable boat to take us out to the sailing sloop. Just to warn you, the water is kind of choppy today."

I patted my thick winter coat. "Waterproof and warm. Although my shoes and jeans, not so much."

"I know what you mean. I keep meaning to buy some of that spray to waterproof my work shoes for this weather." We headed around the corner. "Nate finished the examination. He stands by his first theory that the murder took place around eleven last night. And as you so cleverly surmised, he was struck in the head first."

"So when the murderer wrapped the ribbon around his neck to cut off his oxygen, there was no struggle. Maybe the person did that because they knew they weren't strong enough to fight him off otherwise. It seems that might be a check in the ex-wife column. Which brings me to the ribbon. I saw the carolers in full costume yesterday, and the women had ribbons on their bonnets that looked similar to the ribbon on the victim's neck."

Briggs pulled out his notebook and wrote down the information as we climbed the steps to the wharf.

The morning's grim discovery had cast a shadow over the festivities, and the marina was as quiet as a morgue. (No bad taste humor intended but sometimes it just works.)

I gazed out at the water. "I'm surprised the boats have all stayed anchored at Pickford Beach. I expected them to turn around and head back to their home ports."

"Apparently there was a brief meeting at the mayor's office this morning about the weekend's events. Tonight, the other boat owners are gathering on the beach for a small memorial for Mr. Ruxley, and they've agreed to keep the boats dark."

We had to walk a wide berth around a massive group of gulls and pigeons who were thrilled to have their pier and their fish bits back, free of the people stampede.

"So the light show is over?" I asked.

"No holiday lights tonight. But tomorrow night they are back on. Port Danby is the last stop for the flotilla. Local news crews will be here Saturday to film the activities. The boat owners go to a great deal of trouble and expense for this. It seems they didn't want to miss out on their annual fifteen minutes of fame."

Tim Ruxley, the victim's brother, had toned down his holiday attire, replacing his red Santa hat with a black cap and his reindeer sweater with a plain gray sweatshirt. Timothy had a nicer, less stern looking face than his brother. This afternoon, just hours after learning that his brother was dead, he had a somber but not altogether anguished expression.

Several of the other boat owners were standing with him, hands deep in pockets and faces shielded by the cold with tall coat collars and parka hoods. There was a deep, serious quiet on the beach today, that was for sure. The other boat owners seemed to size up Detective Briggs, almost looking angry about his interference, as we reached the inflatable boat.

One man wearing a fishing hat and a yellow rain slicker stuck around as the others dispersed. "If you're looking for the killer out here on this beach, none of us, not even Tim here, had a beef with

Chad Ruxley. We've all been meeting once a year for this event for ten years and each and every one of us looks forward to the reunion. Chad was as good a guy as any. Even his brother here will tell you that."

Detective Briggs, who never lost his cool, quietly listened to the man's somewhat pinch faced lecture. When the man was finished, my smooth as melted butter detective friend nodded politely.

"I'm truly sorry about your friend, Chad Ruxley. I assure you I'm not out here looking for a killer. I'm out here looking for evidence, anything that might lead us to the person who strangled Mr. Ruxley. It's my job."

"Of course," the man muttered something and was just about to walk away.

"Uh, Mr.—" Briggs waited for the man to fill in the blank.

"Mr. Collins," he said, now looking a little more put off than strident.

"Yes, Mr. Collins." Briggs pulled out his notebook and wrote down the name, which made the man's brows pinch together. "Mr. Collins, if you don't mind, please let the other boat owners know that I'll probably be talking to each one of them at some point today."

Mr. Collins was most assuredly not happy about that, and it seemed he wished he'd kept his earlier opinion to himself. He hurried away.

"Mr. Ruxley, this is my assistant, Miss Pinkerton. She'll be coming along with us."

"Not that I have anything to hide, but don't you need a search warrant to check the boat?"

"I just want to ask you a few questions about your brother and get a look at your boat. I won't be doing any searching. Unless you think I should get a warrant. Then I'll be happy to oblige, but you'll need to commit to staying anchored here for several more days."

"No, I can't commit to that. I need to make arrangements for my brother. He had no other family." He sounded slightly disgusted that the burden fell on him. "Let's go. You can look. I've got nothing to hide."

Tim Ruxley, who was obviously not thrilled about the intrusion on his boat, begrudgingly secured the inflatable raft. Briggs held out his gloved hand for me to take as I stepped inside.

As his fingers squeezed around my hand, I silently cursed the winter weather and the need for gloves.

# CHAPTER 15

*T*he choppy waves splashed against the inflatable boat, but driven as it was by a motor, we managed to go up and over the rambunctious tide with no more than a heavy spray of salty mist. The temperature dropped rapidly out on the ocean, but it seemed to warm up again as we neared the anchored boats.

Tim Ruxley hardly made eye contact with either of his passengers as he kept a keen eye on the surf. Like a true captain, he moved the rudder to steer us safely to the stern of *Cloud Nine*. A ladder was hooked to the railing. Its metal rungs trailed off below the surface of the water. I didn't relish climbing onto the ladder of a boat that was rising and falling with an agitated sea, especially because I was starting out from an inflatable boat that was bobbing on the surface like a beach ball in a pool filled with wild kids.

Mr. Ruxley held the inflatable boat as steady and securely as possible at the stern, while Briggs supported my arm and back. My gloved fingers gripped the metal ladder. It lifted slightly away from the boat as I hoisted myself up and out of the raft. I managed to climb on board without making a fool of myself, and for that, I was thoroughly relieved. Ruxley and Briggs followed at a much breezier pace.

Ruxley was still eyeing me with a decent dollop of suspicion. I decided to make my presence minimal, all the while twitching my nose back and forth hoping to pick up a match to one of the two smells I'd noticed on the victim. It wasn't going to be easy, especially because it had been several hours since I'd breathed in those scents. And since they weren't anything familiar or obvious, they were a little scrambled in my olfactory cells.

Briggs and Tim Ruxley walked to what I believed was referred to as mid ship. They were halfway between the bow and stern. Since the boat was anchored, the sails were down. But the holiday lights and decorations still twittered, shook and swayed with the motion of the sea and the perpetual wind.

Briggs had out his notepad, and the men were deep in conversation. I pretended I was admiring the decorations. They were, as both Lola and Ryder had mentioned, somewhat worn out. The coat of varnish had added a layer of vibrancy back to the original colors on the tall wooden nutcracker, but what he really needed was a complete makeover. I casually leaned next to the nutcracker and breathed in. The varnish was dry. A normal nose would no longer detect any of the volatile molecules but, even muted by the moist, ocean air, I could still smell it.

My shoulders dropped. The pungent chemical fumes clinging to the fibers of Chad Ruxley's sweater and the ribbon did not match the varnish on the Nutcracker. I scooted with small steps here and there to take in deep breaths. Just as the varnish hadn't matched the chemical smell, I couldn't find anything that had a fresh wood scent. The opposite in fact. Even the bits of odor coming off the boat's teak deck smelled more of mildew and stale ocean water than the original wood.

I finished my nasal inspection and returned to where the men were standing. The conversation seemed amiable enough. Tim Ruxley's stiff, defensive posture on the beach had relaxed some. From the bits I could hear, it seemed he was telling Briggs about his relationship with his brother. The general noise on the boat, the churn of the ocean and the intermittent screech of the seagulls out on the water hunting for fish made it impossible for me to hear much.

After a short while, Ruxley leaned to look past Detective Briggs.

Some of that earlier suspicion returned. Briggs and I hadn't taken enough time to define my reason for coming along. It seemed Tim Ruxley was beginning to wonder just what my role was on the case.

Detective Briggs glanced back in the direction of Ruxley's questioning glower. He caught me in a weak, awkward smile, and came to my rescue.

"Mr. Ruxley, Miss Pinkerton is an olfactory expert." I knew he used the scientific terms to make it sound more official. I rather liked the sound of it. "She detected a chemical on your brother's clothing. I brought her along to see if she could find the same scent on your boat."

Briggs shot me a questioning glance. I shook my head to let him know there was no match.

Briggs' sudden admission seemed to fluster Ruxley, and his nostrils widened. He wasn't at all happy about it but then who would be pleased to find out they were under suspicion for killing a sibling. "I think it's time I took you both back to shore," he said tersely.

"Yes, we are done here," Briggs told him. "Although, I might have more questions at another time."

Ruxley's demeanor made me instantly uncomfortable. I fidgeted my feet on the deck, wanting nothing more than to be taken back to shore. I only hoped that Ruxley wouldn't stop halfway and toss us both out. I was sure that notion had gone through his head once or twice.

But Detective Briggs didn't seem the least bit concerned about Ruxley's tense, tight posture and the flaring nostrils. He was, once again, calm and composed. With one exception. Occasionally, and I was sure I was the only person to ever notice it, (which said a lot about how much time I spent looking at the man's face) a tiny muscle in his cheek twitched when he was irritated. It was especially hard to see from the distance I stood and beneath his winter beard stubble, but I was sure I saw it now.

Before taking a step toward the stern, Briggs stopped and looked at Ruxley. "Mr. Ruxley, I will be honest with you, in homicide cases like this, we generally look to a family member or friend first. So, you'll excuse me if this intrusion on your boat has caused you personal offense. You've admitted yourself that you and your brother rarely ever spoke, and you lost a great deal of money when he pushed you out of the family business. I admire your fortitude for getting your business life back on track and congratulations on that. But your brother was brutally murdered in Port Danby, a town that is under my protection. I will find his killer, and I expect complete cooperation from you."

Tim Ruxley's lips twisted and turned as if someone had just shoved a sour lemon in his mouth. He nodded hesitantly and without another word, he brushed past Briggs and me and headed to the stern.

Detective Briggs reached my side and we walked together.

I leaned my head closer to him and whispered, "Boom."

He tapped me with his elbow but kept his face serious as stone.

Ruxley climbed down first to hold the inflatable boat steady, or at least that was what I hoped. Briggs stood by to help me onto the ladder. I gripped the sides and threw my first leg over. As I looked down, I noticed a small piece of fabric fluttering off the rough, splintered edge of the railing. I pointed to it. Briggs leaned over to look at it. It was the same as the khaki fabric from Chad Ruxley's coat. He reached down and pulled it free from the splinter and stuck it in his pocket.

I climbed down into the boat. Briggs quickly joined me. Going with the tide, the ride back to shore was fast and just a touch more thrilling, especially as we rode a steep, churlish wave to shore.

Briggs gave me a hand out of the boat. The buzz of the outboard motor vibrated the air as Ruxley turned right around and headed back toward his boat.

We watched him for a second and then hiked through the wet sand back to the pier.

I stomped my boots on the bottom step to rid them of sand. "It seems Mr. Ruxley is not our biggest fan."

Briggs shook off his boots as well. "You noticed that too. Most people aren't too friendly when they think they are under suspicion for murder. Their parting of ways in business happened quite a few years ago. Ruxley Plumbing had been handed down to Chad Ruxley, the eldest son. Tim was treated like a partner, but he was never a partner on paper. And when they had a falling out ten years ago, Tim left the company for good. They rarely spoke anymore. He admits he chose the company name T. Ruxley Plumbing just to aggravate his older brother. But they operate in different parts of the country, so I don't think it's been a problem. And I couldn't get much out of him about his brother's divorce. He claimed not to know why or how it fell apart."

The wharf was still unusually quiet. I wondered if anyone would even show up tomorrow night for the news crews and the light show. It seemed no one wanted to think about something as unpleasant as murder in the peak of the holiday season.

We continued on to Pickford Way. "Did he say what the falling out was about?"

Briggs pulled the zipper up higher on his coat. "He was pretty vague. Said it was just the usual sibling rivalry stuff."

"Like a table war?"

He looked over at me with the cutest look of confusion.

I laughed. "I've never had a sibling, but the geography of my shop, located between Elsie and Lester, is giving me a pretty good idea of what sibling rivalry looks like."

"Ah, I see. Is that why every time I go to have a coffee or a muffin, they've added some new trinket of luxury to the sidewalk tables?"

"You've noticed?"

He shrugged. "It's kind of nice to have your rear end cradled in a soft cushion while you're drinking coffee."

We stopped in front of the police station. "Well, I guess I'll take off my detective hat and put back on my florist hat."

"Thank you for letting me borrow your nose for the afternoon."

"Anytime. I'm just sorry Evangeline couldn't be more help." I blinked up at him for his reaction. He shook his head. "You're right. It's too long." I was just about to walk away. The awkwardly silent ride back to the shore had pushed the last moments on deck from my mind. "Wait," I said. "What about the fabric? Isn't that the missing piece from Chad Ruxley's coat?"

"I'd say so. I'm going to go check the coat right now."

"Is it important?" I asked with an edge of optimism.

"I don't think so. All it does is verify that Chad Ruxley climbed onto his brother's boat. His coat probably got caught on a splinter of wood. We already knew he'd gone aboard because you saw it happen."

My shoulders sank. "That's makes sense, unfortunately. Good day, Detective Briggs."

"Good day, Miss Pinkerton."

# CHAPTER 16

$\mathcal{R}$yder was sitting at the island eating a sandwich and thumbing through his phone as I walked out of my office.

"You finally stopped for lunch." I started picking up the floral scraps from the work table. "I've got everything ordered for the holiday bouquets and the dinner table arrangements. And I think there's enough if we want to take in four or five more orders. Then we'll have to cut them off. I've got at least thirty orders in the stack. We won't have enough time or supplies to fill many more than that before Christmas."

"Thirty orders? Wow, that's good."

Ryder had taped paper over the window on both sides now shielding it from all eyes, even mine.

"I can't wait to see the window." I stared at him hopefully, but he finished his sandwich and pretended not to hear me.

"I guess that means I won't see it until it's done."

He flicked his bangs away from his eyes and grinned at me. "Yep."

The bell rang, and Kate Upton sashayed into the store. Sashay was the only way to describe the exaggerated hip swing Kate was tossing around in her skin tight paisley leggings and equally tight sweater. Kate, the owner of the stylish Mod Frock clothing boutique, was a fashion icon around town. Today she had pulled together her snug but groovy look with short black boots and giant silver hoop earrings.

"Hello, Kate, how can I help you?"

Kate strode to the kissing bough and stared up at it. I shot a curious glance at Ryder, who seemed to be wondering, with some concern, if she was expecting a kiss.

She pointed up at the sphere of holly. "How much for that?"

"The kissing bough?" I asked, still slightly baffled. "I have the frames for two more, but it'll take me a few days. You can pick the decorations and ribbons—"

Kate shook her head and her long curtain of bangs swayed across her forehead. She always had different hair color and had opted for a dark sable brown this week. "I need one today. How much for this one?"

"Oh, well, I hadn't put a price on it because I thought I'd keep it in the shop."

"How much did you charge Lola?"

Now I at least knew where she had gotten the idea for a kissing bough in her shop. Even though I'd made Lola a kissing bough as a gesture of friendship, I hated to show too much favoritism to any of the shop owners. "Twenty?" I said too much like a question.

"I'll pay you thirty for this one, and I need one more for home. I can pick up the second one in a few days. My winter party isn't for another week. But I want to hang this one in my shop today. Can your assistant come down and hang it for me?"

Ryder looked my direction waiting for me to answer, but I'd looked his way to see if I could get a sense of whether or not he wanted to do it. We both stared blankly at each other for a moment.

"If Ryder doesn't mind, he can bring it down to your shop and hang it for you."

"I don't mind," Ryder said.

The bell rang and Lola walked inside. Without a word to anyone, she went straight through the store and directly into my office. Something she had never done before. Kate didn't seem to notice as she searched through her purple clutch purse for her money. Unfortunately, Ryder definitely took notice and he looked hurt by Lola's rather rude entrance.

"Ryder, would you please write up a receipt for Miss Yardley and take down the order for the second kissing bough?" I backed up toward my office and motioned over my shoulder with my thumb. "I need to attend to something in my office."

I turned around and ducked into the teensy office space I'd carved out from a walk-in storage closet. Lola pinched and rubbed her chin as she paced the eight foot floor, which meant a lot of back and forth and a lot of snow puddles from her boots.

"What's wrong, Lola?"

"Nothing," she said in a tone that clearly meant something was wrong.

"You just swept through my store like a hurricane, not even taking the time to say hello to anyone, and now your are creating a lake of melted snow in my office. Something must be wrong."

Lola grumbled a sigh and walked around my desk to sit in my chair.

"Make yourself comfy." I leaned against the rolling cart where I kept my office supplies and order forms. "What's up?" I asked the question, already knowing this had to do with the construction guy.

My chair squeaked as she sat abruptly forward and showed me her phone. "Not one call or text. Not even a blip. We had a such a great time on the carriage ride and then we talked and laughed and—"

"Shared pancakes at Franki's, yes I know. That was just last night. Not a month ago. Give him some time. And—"

This time she cut me off. "Don't jump into one of your lectures about how if it's meant to be blah, blah, blah."

I couldn't see my own face, but I was certain it looked exactly like my mom's face when I used to flippantly wave off her advice. And in retrospect, most of that advice was good. "Fine, Lola. No lecture. But I'm afraid there's not much I can do or say. You'll just have to wait for him to call. If he's out on Beacon Cliffs at a construction site, he probably doesn't have reception or the time to make a call."

She slapped her hand on the desk. "You're so right. See, that's why I came here to regain my rational thoughts."

"You mean from the friend who says, 'blah, blah, blah'?" Naturally I added in the talking hand puppet for visual aid.

Her dark red lashes fluttered down in shame. "I'm sorry. You never say blah, blah and you are right again. I was just frustrated."

"And impatient."

"And acting like a junior in high school," she added as if she'd read my mind. She hopped up and circled around the desk. "Which gives me an idea, so now I need to ask you a favor."

"Why do I feel like this isn't going to head in a good direction?"

"How about taking a little drive out to Beacon Cliffs? I'll buy you an afternoon latte for the road."

"You must be kidding?"

Lola grabbed my hands. "Please. The entire thing won't take longer than thirty minutes, long enough for you to drink a mocha latte."

"I've got stuff to do. Besides, Ryder has gone down the block to hang the kissing bough for Kate, which is your fault for coming up with such a brilliant idea. And by the way, if Kate asks—you paid me twenty dollars for yours. And why do you need me at all? Just drive by, spy on the man and head back home."

"I'm not spying so much as checking to see if he's still alive and well. If he was sick or dead it would give him a good excuse for not calling me. Plus, I need you to drive so I can duck in case he sees us."

The goat bell rang. "See, I can't go. I've got a customer."

Lola's loud, discouraged footsteps sounded behind me as I walked to the front of the shop. Ryder was putting away the step ladder. "I was just about to let you know I was back. It only took a second to hang the sphere."

"Oh good," Lola spoke up from behind.

Ryder's head popped my direction. He brushed his bangs away from his eyes. "Lola," he said with a quick breath, "I didn't see you there. Thought you were gone already."

Lola grabbed my hand. "Nope, just came by to invite Pink out for an afternoon coffee break. You can handle the shop for thirty minutes, can't you?"

I shot her a sideways glance to let her know I was less than thrilled about the whole idea.

"Yeah, no problem. I've got to put a few finishing touches on the window. Go take your coffee break, boss. I've got it covered."

"I won't be more than a half hour." I looked at Lola with a scowl as I said it. "Do you want something from the Coffee Hutch, Ryder?"

"Nope, I'm good. Enjoy."

# CHAPTER 17

$\mathcal{B}$eacon Cliffs, our spying destination, was just off Highway 48, the two lane thoroughfare between Port Danby and the larger, neighboring town of Chesterton. Beacon Cliffs was a tiny neighborhood of large, posh beach houses that sat on a section of coast with a million dollar view of the ocean. Steep gray cliffs and tall evergreens shielded the exclusive neighborhood from the rest of civilization.

I turned onto the road leading to Beacon Cliffs. The houses were just a few miles away.

I lifted my cup from the holder and took a sip. "Hmm, Lester put in an extra squirt of chocolate, and it's really hitting the spot. Which reminds me, you're still going to Elsie's tonight for truffle making, right?"

"I forgot. Is that tonight?"

"Lola, you know Elsie's been planning this for weeks. We're going to eat cheese and crackers, sip wine and then immerse our hands in melted chocolate. We're even going to put in Elsie's 'I Love Lucy' DVDs and watch the chocolate factory episode to get in the mood. I'm looking forward to it. And if you don't come, I'm not sharing any truffles with you. It's your call."

"Is that a form of chocolate blackmail?" She scooted down suddenly. "Look, the construction site is at the entrance to the neighborhood."

"That's lucky. I was wondering how I would drive my chirpy, shabby little car through a neighborhood of Cadillacs and Porsches and not be noticed."

Lola pulled her black felt slouch hat low over her head to hide her red hair. She slumped low enough that the seatbelt ran across her chin. "We should have turned off the defrost, so the windows would be foggy."

"Of course. I prefer to drive a car where I can't see in any direction. It sort of adds that element of surprise to the trip."

"I think that latte had too much caffeine. It's making you kind of mean."

"Yes, it's the caffeine."

Lola's face snapped my direction. She peered up at me from under the floppy brim of her hat. "Did you just do an eye roll. I thought I heard it."

"Sorry, I'll work on keeping my eye rolls quieter."

We came up to the section of street just ahead of the construction site. A bright yellow banner with the words "Dayton Construction" was stretched across the chain link fence that bordered most of the site. The massive wooden frame of what looked to be a gigantic, boxy house stood in the center of a dirt lot. It was hard to tell where windows and doors would go, but from the silhouette created by the lumber, it looked like the new house was going to lack something very important to make it a home—character.

"I guess it's all about size and space in some of these big houses," I said. "It looks like an ugly mansion at this stage in the game."

"Yeah, who needs a mansion? Think of how much cleaning you'd have to do. But I guess they hire people for that." Lola sprang up and then slouched back down. "I think that's him in the bright yellow hat."

"If you hadn't noticed, they are all wearing yellow hats."

"The tall guy with the broad shoulders. The one right next to the trailer."

I had to tilt my head some to see him. Thankfully, he didn't seem to notice the two women staring at him from the road. A large pond-sized puddle of water had collected at the base of the portable metal steps up to the construction trailer. Randall Dayton looked back as someone whistled. He yelled something back and then plowed through the puddle to the steps.

"Look how he just marched through that water," Lola said as if she was describing someone saving a litter of puppies from a burning building.

"So brave," I said with an appropriate head shake.

"Oh stop. It's just that when we had pie at the diner on our first date, his new shoes were soaked. He said he had been too busy to waterproof them. He must have found time." She turned to me.

I blinked back at her, to let her know I didn't need to hear anything else about his shoes or puddles. She was talking about him and their pie date as if they'd had many experiences together. I was worried that she was getting way too past herself on this one.

"I need to go back, Lola. We've seen him. He's alive and well but obviously very busy." I turned the car around and headed back toward the highway. "What city is Dayton Construction based out of? Sometimes, if the contract is big enough, like with this mansion, a construction company will go out of their way to build it. Literally."

She slowly sat back up in the seat and pushed up the hat. "What do you mean?"

"I mean, these guys are out here working but their home base, or home towns might be several hundred miles away. Which means once this house is built, the crew will go back home."

"You just love to smother my romantic dreams, Pink."

"No, I'm just putting that possibility out there."

"Yeah, yeah. I get your point. I'll have to ask him next time I see him." She slumped back down. "*If* I see him again."

# CHAPTER 18

*A*fter my time trip back into the high school years where driving past a boy's house was foolish but entirely acceptable, I finished up my work in the shop. Ryder had left early. He'd earned it. He hadn't revealed the window to me yet, and he made me promise not to peek behind the paper curtain. I'd seen enough of it to know it would be wonderful. I was going to have to give him a nice holiday bonus. He hadn't been working long at the shop, but he had already made himself a valuable employee. I wanted to keep him happy.

I turned out the lights and headed out of the shop. I had a few hours to feed pets, take a bath and relax before heading over to Elsie's for truffle making. I hadn't heard from Lola, but I expected her to join us. Although, I was under no illusions. I knew if Randall Dayton called or texted, asking for a date, she'd break our plans like a brittle toothpick.

A car rolled up and stopped in front of the shop. I was still locking my front door when I heard Detective Briggs call my name.

I turned around and walked to his car. He stepped out so I didn't have to bend down to speak through the window.

"I saw your lights on so I headed this way." He pulled off his hat as he looked down at my purse. "But I see you're on your way home for the night." He was about to say something else but hesitated.

"What is it, Detective Briggs? Do you need me to help with some evidence? I was on my way home, but I have a few hours before I need to be somewhere else."

His brown eyes took on an apologetic glaze. "I'm sorry. This is— what's the word I'm looking for—untoward, I think about sums it up. I hate to cut into your time again, but I'm heading out to Mayfield Beach. The Christmas caroling group is camping there, and I need to speak to Chad Ruxley's ex-wife. I interviewed some of the other boat owners and possibly found the last two people to see him alive. Vick and Max are two retired teachers on the pleasure boat anchored next to Ruxley's *Sea Gem*. They said that Ruxley was sitting along the starboard railing, chatting across the water with them when Ruxley got a text. He told them he had to row to shore because his ex-wife, Charlene, needed to talk to him. They said he joked about her always needing money but that he seemed anxious to meet her. Max insisted that Chad was still pining for his ex."

"Poor man. Poor man," I said louder as I straightened my posture. "Do you think she killed him?"

"Well, the text explains what he was doing up on the pier at that hour. And then there's the matter of the ribbons you mentioned. The forensic tests on the fibers of the ribbon and sweater needed to be sent to another lab. We don't have sophisticated enough technology in our local lab for traces of evidence. And since we aren't exactly sure what we're looking for—"

I reached forward and touched his gloved hand. "Detective Briggs, it's fine. I don't need an explanation. You'd like me to sniff around their campsite and see if anything comes up a match."

"I don't want to cut into your time any more than I already have, but I'm running up against a wall with this case. And much like the Marian Fitch case, I'm short on time. There are a lot of strangers in town for this event. I need to figure this out before people disappear."

"Again, you don't need to say anything else to convince me. You forget a million little adrenaline receptors light up in my brain when you ask me to look for evidence. Millicent is ready." I tapped my nose. "Gosh, that one is awful." Briggs opened the passenger door for me. "Maybe just Milli," I suggested.

I heard his deep laugh outside the car as he circled around to the driver's side. Seconds later we were off to the Mayfield campsite.

"So the physical evidence is scarce so far? I guess with this weather, fingerprints are masked by gloves, and even footprints don't stick around long in the mushy snow and ice on the pier."

"Physical evidence is lacking. We haven't been able to find his phone either. He didn't have it on him, and it was nowhere on the pier or on his boat. Possible motives have been elusive too. Chad doesn't seem to have any enemies. The other boat owners knew him in varying degrees, but everyone genuinely liked the man. They praised him for being honest and having a great deal of integrity. Apparently, he was quite generous and always picked up the tab at social nights out. He gave his wife half of everything when they split, and the split supposedly came from her. Irreconcilable differences is what the divorce record states. Everyone knew that the two brothers didn't have a relationship anymore, but none of the other boat owners ever saw much animosity between them."

"I sure did," I noted.

"Yes, that seemed to be an unusual event. Or at least according to the other captains."

"Do you think it's possible they are just trying to squash any ugly rumors? This will certainly put a damper on future light flotillas. Maybe they just want it to fade away without much bad publicity for the event. Then by next Christmas, it will all be forgotten."

Briggs had put on a black fedora hat to guard against the nightly chill. It pushed his slightly longish hair up high against his collar. With the hat and his black overcoat, he reminded me of one of those tough talking detectives from the mid twentieth century, the kind who went relentlessly after the dangerous gangsters.

"You and I think a lot alike, Miss Pinkerton," he said in his usual gentlemanly way, which quickly dispelled the vision I had of him as a tough talking gangster chaser.

"Do we? So you were thinking the same thing about the other boat owners? That they're covering up to keep their event pristine?"

"Pretty much. But I could be wrong. I'm hoping the ex-wife, my second person of interest, will lead us to a few more solid clues."

"In that case—" I said as I pulled off my gloves.

"What are you doing? It'll be plenty cold down by the beach."

"I have no doubt of that, but I can't very well go sniffing around a campsite without looking like a hungry bear. If I run my hand over surfaces, I can sometimes pick up a scent. But it doesn't work with thick gloves."

"Makes sense. You really are good at this."

I couldn't contain my grin. "I'm learning from the best."

He didn't hold back his grin either.

The larger coastal town of Mayfield was to the east of Port Danby. It shared the same stretch of beach with our town, but their stretch was much longer. In my biased opinion, I didn't think Mayfield had nearly as much charm as Port Danby. One section of the public beach and a good portion of the forested land leading up to the beach had been designated as a campsite.

Detective Briggs pulled his car into the parking lot where travelers with motor homes could hook their vehicles up to water and electricity. There were only five motor homes parked in the camp. The carolers' motor homes were easy to spot because they had their group name, The Merry Carolers, painted across the back of each vehicle.

A woman and a man were sitting at a picnic table in front of the motor homes. The man was browsing through a magazine and finishing up a hot dog. The woman, interestingly enough, was doing some kind of repair on her bonnet. The two singers looked very different dressed in sweatshirts and jeans. Because of her red hair and ample cheeks, I recognized the woman immediately as the caroler with the fur trimmed mantelet.

The man saw us walking toward them and stood, looking uneasy about the prospect of two strangers approaching their campsite.

Briggs pulled his badge from his pocket. "Good evening. I'm Detective Briggs of the Port Danby Police, and this is Miss Pinkerton."

"I'm Jonah Iverton." The man was long and thin everywhere except for his belly. It almost looked as if he'd swallowed a bowling ball. His defensive stance softened but only slightly. "How can we help you?"

The woman sitting at the table had a bonnet and a spool of ribbon in front of her. It was tartan ribbon, exactly like the one wrapped around Chad Ruxley's neck. I sensed that Briggs noticed the coincidence as well. He stared at the ribbon before turning his attention back to Jonah.

"I was hoping to talk to Charlene Ruxley. I'm working on her husband's murder case."

"Ex-husband," the woman with round cheeks piped up quickly. She put down the bottle of glue she was holding and lifted her hand to shake and introduce herself. I made a point to stick out my hand first. I was hoping there would be just enough scent left on her palm from the glue bottle. It was a long shot, but it couldn't hurt to try. Especially with a possible piece of the murder weapon sitting right in front of us curled in a pretty bow waiting to be glued to the bonnet.

She was slightly put off by my forthrightness, but she took my hand. "I'm Kendra. Charlene has gone off on an errand. She should be back soon."

"Or maybe you should just come back tomorrow." Jonah was far less congenial than Kendra.

"We'll wait a few minutes, if you don't mind," Briggs suggested. Jonah responded with a half-hearted nod and then walked back inside the motor home. I discretely rubbed my nose with my hand. There was no match. It was a water-based glue with no toxic or chemical odor.

"Miss—" Briggs waited for her to fill in the blank.

"Mrs. Olson," Kendra noted.

"Mrs. Olson, is it possible for me to get just an inch or two of that ribbon?"

Kendra's mouth dropped open, and a puff of breath hovered in the chilly air in front of her face. She, of course, had no idea why he wanted it and was no doubt stunned that a detective would be interested in her ribbon.

She finally pulled her mouth into a smile. "I'm not sure it will go with your severe black coat, but what do I know?" She chuckled and picked up the scissors to snip off a piece of ribbon.

"Thank you so much." Detective Briggs placed the piece of ribbon in his pocket. Then he walked away, pretending to make a phone call, but I knew he was scouting around, looking for something, anything that might point him toward the killer.

"I saw the group in full costume singing in Port Danby." I said cheerily to Kendra. "Such a beautiful wardrobe and so lively and authentic."

"Thank you." Kendra lifted her bonnet for me to get a better look under the dim lights of the campground. "We fashion it all from actual Victorian clothing. I just love the skirts and bonnets. Makes me feel as if I've stepped into another world."

I smiled. "Same for those of us watching your performance. It was truly wonderful. There are five of you, right?"

"Yes. Bobby and Rita got tired of the campsite and went to dinner."

I motioned to the bottle of glue. "What happened? Wardrobe malfunction?"

She found my comment amusing. "I suppose in a way. Somewhere in the hustle and bustle, I lost the ribbon off my bonnet. Fortunately, we had an extra spool of this tartan ribbon. It's my favorite and it works best with the colors of my skirt and mantelet."

"Yes, the cherry red mantelet with the white fur trim? It's lovely."

"Thank you. I had my seamstress recreate one from an old Victorian fashion plate."

"I heard your group singing on Thursday night. How late did you have to perform? It got too cold for me by nine. I can't imagine how hard it is to sing for hours in frigid weather."

"The costumes keep us warm. Since that was the only night of our performance—" She briefly frowned to show that she was saddened by the tragedy. "I can remember exactly how long we sang. We caroled until ten o'clock and then took the horse and carriage back to Jonah's car. We always tow a car behind each motor home when we travel. It gives us the freedom to move around towns easily without acting like a bunch of slow turtles with our houses on our backs."

Headlights temporarily lit up the campsite. "Ah here's Charlene now. She left last night's performance an hour early. She had a terrible headache, and the cold air and crowds were making it worse."

Detective Briggs had returned to our conversation just as Kendra mentioned Charlene leaving early with a headache. "What time was that?" he asked, suddenly, startling Kendra who had not heard him walk up.

"Oh, hello, detective. We ended around ten, so Charlene must have left around nine." She moved her round chin back and forth in thought. "Yes, it was right after Silent Night."

Charlene Ruxley climbed out of her car. She was younger than I expected. With her turned up nose and wide set eyes she reminded me of my third grade teacher, Miss Langley, who was gentle, kind and fun. She had two pet hamsters in her classroom named Atticus and Scout. I got up extra early for school every day in third grade because I couldn't wait to get to Miss Langley's class.

Briggs went straight into detective mode, showing her his badge and letting her know he had a few questions. He glanced back at Kendra, who seemed to get the hint.

She stood up quickly. "I'll just head inside then. It was nice meeting you, Miss Pinkerton, Detective Briggs."

Kendra disappeared inside the motor home.

Charlene hugged herself against the cold and possibly against a case of nerves. It was hard to tell. But she was underdressed for the weather, clad only in a sweater, jeans and a knitted shawl.

"What can I do for you, Detective Briggs? I was waiting for someone from the station to come and interview me. I thought it would be earlier, during the day."

"Yes, I'm sorry for the late visit," Briggs said as he pulled out his notebook. "This is Miss Pinkerton. She is working on the case with me."

(Oh heart be still.)

"I haven't seen Chad in six months. Even this weekend, I managed to somehow avoid him. I saw his boat, of course. But we never passed each other. Not even on the pier."

Briggs scribbled away with his pen. "Is that why you texted him on Thursday night? So you two could meet up and talk?"

Her stunned silence pulled Briggs' gaze away from his notebook. "Ms. Ruxley?"

"Ms. Carlton, please. It's my maiden name. I just haven't had time to change it back legally. I'm not sure what you mean. What text? Did you find my phone?"

Briggs turned some of the pages of his notebook back. "Two other boat owners said they were talking to Chad around ten o'clock when he got a text. He told them you had texted that you needed to talk to him. He left immediately to the pier." Her last question had finally caught up with him. "Why did you ask if we found your phone?"

"It's gone. It sort of negates being dressed in Victorian costumes when a twenty-first century cell phone rings in your pocket. We leave our phones, keys and other things like extra props—caroling books, candles, bells—in two canvas bags close to where we're singing. Then we can easily carry everything with us to our next location. I left the performance early last night. I had a terrible migraine, and the cold was making it worse. The canvas bags were tucked behind the bike rental kiosk during our performance on the wharf. I went to get my keys and phone. I rummaged through both bags but couldn't find my phone. I figured I'd left it back in the motor home. My head hurt so bad, I didn't even think about it. I got back to the motor home and climbed into bed. I still couldn't find my phone this morning."

"When you got your keys, did anything seem amiss with the canvas bags?" Briggs asked.

"Our stuff had been moved around. Not a lot, just slightly. Nothing appeared to be missing. Again, I wasn't thinking clearly with the migraine. But there were so many people, it seems entirely possible that someone could have slipped into the kiosk and rummaged through the bag. But nothing else was missing. Just my phone. Excuse me." Charlene pulled an intricately embroidered handkerchief from her pocket and wiped her nose. "This cold air always gives me the sniffles." She refolded the square of white linen.

"It's unusual to see an embroidered handkerchief these days," I noted. "I guess it goes well with your Victorian era costumes."

"I embroider them myself." She proudly unfolded it. Red and green poinsettias were hand-stitched in one corner of the handkerchief. "I'll be selling some at our table tomorrow night. On our last night of caroling, we set up a table with our music CDs, song books, bells and other goodies. It's nice extra income and helps pay for our travels."

"Soup is ready, Charlene," Jonah called out the side window of the motor home.

"If there's nothing else, Detective Briggs. I've got dinner waiting."

"Yes, of course," he said. "Have a good evening."

We headed back to his car. Once inside, I slipped my hands back into my gloves. "No match on the glue and I touched the picnic benches just to check for wood smell or varnish. I found nothing. It seems I'm not much help to you."

"Not true at all," he insisted, but I was having trouble convincing myself.

"I guess that sort of takes the heat off of her." I fastened my seat belt. "Since her phone was stolen the night she supposedly texted Chad to meet her on the pier."

Briggs checked the side mirror and pulled out onto the road. "Yes. Unless, of course, she disposed of the phone and made up the story about it being stolen because she knew the text would implicate her."

"Ah ha," I nodded. "And that's why you're the detective and I'm just the occasional assistant with a talented nose. What about Victoria? Too royal for a nose?"

Briggs smiled as he turned the car and headed back to Port Danby.

# CHAPTER 19

$\mathcal{L}$ola's car was already parked out front of Elsie's house. Elsie had lined her walkway with giant wooden candy canes, and her entire porch was strung with snowflake shaped twinkling lights. I could smell melted chocolate the second I stepped out of the car. The pungent, slightly sweet smell of chimney smoke curling up from nearly every chimney on the street muted some of the rich cocoa smell, but it was still strong enough to make my mouth water.

Elsie opened the door wearing a yellow and blue checked apron and one of her usual flashy smiles. "Thank goodness you're here. Now maybe droopy drawers will cheer up."

"I heard that," Lola called from the kitchen as I stepped into Elsie's house.

Elsie laughed. "Oops. Anyhow, come on in and we can get started. We need to coat the truffles. Then we'll watch Lucy and nibble cheese and crackers while they harden."

Lola had perched herself on a stool at the kitchen counter. She'd knotted her curly hair in a careless knot at the back of her head.

Lola took a sip of wine and then lowered her glass to the counter. "Good thing you tied your hair back, Pink. The iron fisted chef, here, told me I had to get my red mop tied up or it would get in the way of the truffles."

Elsie poured me a glass of wine and ignored Lola's comment. Which was probably for the best. I'd been looking forward to the evening, and I'd hate for it to go south before we'd even dipped our hands in chocolate.

I took a sip of wine. "I thought Lester might join us."

"Les? No. He's been busy at his house." Elsie shook her head. "My silly brother has talked himself into remodeling his bathroom." She laughed between sips of wine. "He ripped out everything, right down to the studs. And get this, he's putting in one of those deep soak tubs. This cold winter air has reminded him both of how old he is and how much his years as a fireman destroyed his back and joints. Lots of arthritis."

"Neat. I wish I had a soak tub," I said.

Lola laughed. "I can just picture Les sitting in a tub of bubbles with scented candles lit all around him." She lifted her glass to her mouth but froze halfway. "Ooh yuck, now I'm trying to erase that image."

Elsie walked to her refrigerator. "Now he's at that point of no return on the project. I promised to bring him some truffles tomorrow."

I walked into the kitchen. Sitting on a piece of wax paper on Elsie's white quartz counter was the biggest slab of milk chocolate I had ever seen. Two large chunks had been broken off. Elsie turned from the refrigerator with a tray filled with small chocolate balls.

"This is a massive bar of chocolate, Elsie. Where did you get it?"

"From my chocolate supplier. It's special order. They have a ten pound bar mold."

"Can I just start nibbling from this end?" I laughed at my joke and turned to see if Lola found it funny. She was busy looking at her phone.

"I don't know why I care anyhow," Lola blurted. She was apparently starting a conversation in the middle. Elsie and I stared back at her, baffled by her statement.

Lola glanced up and saw us looking at her expectantly. "I mean about Randall Dayton. Why should I care if he doesn't call? He doesn't live in the area, and he smells like tobacco." She put the phone down. "That's it. I'm done whining about him."

"That's good to hear," I said, not totally convinced by her declaration.

Elsie stretched out some wax paper. "I don't know why you'd be interested in some stranger when the most wonderful guy in the world works right across the street from you."

Lola stared at her with pinched brows. "I adore Lester and his cool Hawaiian shirts, but he's a little old for me."

"Oh stop," Elsie said. "You know very well I'm talking about Ryder."

Elsie looked to me for back up. I shook my head to let her know I was staying clear of the topic.

"Ryder is a great guy," Lola said as she climbed off the stool. "But I don't think he's my type."

"And why not?" Elsie continued . . . unfortunately. "Too perfect?"

Lola waved off her comment. "Let's get this party started. I want to drown my sorrows in melted chocolate."

"Good idea," I said. "I'm kind of disappointed I didn't get to see you make the filling."

I took a sniff. "Hmm, chocolate and whipped cream and vanilla," I declared.

"Exactly right," Elsie said. "And a bit of salt but I guess even your nose can't smell that. I put large chunks of chocolate in the top of this double boiler. The water below heats up so the chocolate melts slowly. You have to be careful with chocolate. If it gets too hot, it separates and seizes up. Then it's ruined. And you don't want to get any water or moisture in it either. After the filling chocolate melted, I folded it into some unsweetened whipped cream. Then I refrigerated it and shaped it into balls. Now it's time to coat them. Let me demonstrate."

Elsie poured some of the melted chocolate from the top of the double boiler out on a clean spot on her counter. She raked the chocolate puddle back and forth with the edge of a spatula. Then she reached into a bowl of solid grated chocolate and sprinkled it on the melted puddle.

"Why are you doing that?" I asked.

"This is called tempering. Adding some cold chocolate will help make the coating shiny and even. Otherwise, it can look dull and get a waxy haze on it." Elsie worked as she narrated. "I gently pick up a tiny ball of chocolate and roll it back and forth until its coated completely. You have to work fast so the center doesn't get too mushy. Then I return it to its spot on the wax paper." She swirled the melted chocolate once around the top to give the truffle a decorative finish.

"You make it look so easy," I marveled. "But I'm ready." I pushed back my sleeves to wash my hands.

"Me too," Lola said.

Elsie handed us each a spoon with her clean hand. "First, I suggest you each take a spoonful of melted chocolate. It helps keep you from wanting to lick your fingers in the middle of coating the candy. Trust me. It's a trick I taught myself years ago. That and always keep one hand clean because the second you coat both hands with chocolate, your nose will have a terrible itch."

Lola and I turned to the pot with our spoons. I felt like a kid stealing a spoonful of cookie dough from my mom's mixing bowl. We both closed our eyes for a second as we coated our tongues with rich, melted chocolate.

"That's heaven," Lola muttered. There was a bit of chocolate at each corner of her mouth as she smiled. "I'm glad you talked me into this."

"I'm glad you came. After all, who needs men when there is melted chocolate, wine and good friends to enjoy."

# CHAPTER 20

*I*'d arrived home after truffle making more intoxicated on chocolate than on the wine. Even though I was a little bleary eyed from the long day and lightheaded from the sugar rush, I had made a firm decision to add more twinkling lights to my porch. My house had looked drab and dreary compared to Elsie's winter wonderland.

Ryder had texted that he would open the shop because he had a few more details to add to the window. He insisted I take the morning off and with my chocolate hangover, I wasn't about to argue the point. The free morning had given me time to search through my closet for my spare Christmas lights. Unfortunately, I hadn't taken much care with them when I had yanked them off my city apartment balcony. I had to waste my precious time untangling them from a knotted ball.

I sat on the bench on my porch, working out the knots and watching Kingston take a much needed flight around the neighborhood. The poor bird really hated the winter months when the trees were more laden with snow and ice than leaves and edible treats.

While I worked, two cars sped along Myrtle Place, each filled to capacity with passengers. More out-of-towners intrigued by the murder-suicide in the big gothic mansion on the hill. I'd been so busy

I hadn't had time to think much about the startling information I'd discovered about the case. It seemed to me that there was no way Bertram Hawksworth had taken his own life. That meant someone else had shot him and then placed the gun in his right hand to make it look like a suicide. And that someone had most likely killed the rest of the family as well. It was not a murder-suicide. It was a murder. A cold, tragic murder and the officer who was first at the scene had figured that out himself before being sent off to a different precinct.

The sharp thwack of a hammer rang out. The sound ricocheted off the houses across the street and bounced back to my side. I put down the thread of lights and walked over to Dash's house. Captain sat on the bottom step, his tail wagging in rhythm with the hammer as Dash pounded a piece of wood to the new porch overhang.

Dash reached for another nail and noticed his audience of one had doubled. "Howdy, neighbor," he called down from the step ladder. He hopped off.

"I don't want to stop you. I just came to watch a tradesman at work."

He blew air from his lips. "Tradesman, I wish. I'll just be happy if the thing is level and stays standing in a wind storm. What are you up to this morning?"

"Well, Elsie's picture worthy holiday decorations made me feel ashamed. So I'm trying to add some more zip to my porch. Only I'm spending most of my time trying to unzip the lights from each other."

Dash laughed. "Ah yes, the annual untangling of the holiday lights. I know it well. My dad used to get so frustrated, he'd just start hanging them up in knotted clusters. All you need is one of those Victorian kissing boughs like you made for Kate's shop."

"You saw that? So you were in her shop and under the kissing bough too?" I shouldn't have been disappointed, but I was definitely feeling a hint of it.

"Next week is my sixteen-year-old niece's birthday. I'm terrible at picking gifts for her. And my sister warned me no gift cards because they are too impersonal. Of course, she didn't give me any good suggestions either, so I called Kate. She told me to come down to the shop, and we'd find something for her. We settled on a shiny pair of boots and a vintage denim jacket. I think Riley is going to love it."

"I sure would if I was sixteen." Suddenly Kate's urgent need for the kissing bough was explained. She was expecting a visit from Dash. I looked up at him. "Did the mistletoe draped kissing bough work its magic while you were shopping?"

"If that's your roundabout way of asking if I kissed Kate while I was there, then sorry to disappoint you. Your kissing bough isn't as magical as you might think."

I released a breath that I hadn't realized I'd been holding. Was I interested in Dash? Or was I not thrilled with the idea of Kate having him? Sometimes a woman's mind was as tangled as a ball of Christmas lights.

Dash walked past me and picked up several planks of wood. He headed back with his load and stopped in front of me. "Just to be clear, Lacey, there's nothing between Kate and me. She was just helping with a perfect gift."

"That's all right, Dash. It's none of my business. I'm going to take my nosy nose and head back to my knotted ball of lights." I turned and caught a whiff of the fresh lumber he was holding. "The woodsy smell," I muttered.

"Yep, that's because it's wood."

"No, I know. That's it. That's the smell I was trying to find. What kind of wood is it?"

"Douglas Fir. It's the most popular wood for building lumber." He pushed his nose close to it. "I don't smell a thing."

"No, it's faint. But it's there. Thank you for this." I headed back toward my house.

"For what?" he called.

"For having lumber for me to smell."

# CHAPTER 21

*M*y elation about recognizing the woodsy smell on Chad Ruxley's sweater had waned a few minutes after my discovery. The odor had been so faint, and it had been long enough that I felt I needed to smell the sweater again just to be sure. And even then, I wasn't sure how it would help solve the crime.

Kingston had decided to take a longer than anticipated journey around the neighborhood. I had to resort to standing on the front porch loudly eating peanuts to get his attention and lure him back to the house. The entire pet trick made me almost miss the window judging.

I jumped out of my car and raced into the shop. Ryder looked miffed about me being so late.

"I'm so sorry, Ryder." I held up the container of truffles I packed for him. "Candy for you." I placed the chocolates on the counter and continued with my apology. "Kingston wouldn't come home, and I didn't want to leave him out in this cold weather. I thought I was going to have to rub hardboiled eggs on my head to get him back into the house."

Ryder opened the container and bit into a truffle. "Man, that's delicious. Good ole, Kingston." He smiled. My story and the peace offering of truffles had washed away any anger. "I miss that bird." He walked over to the paper curtain. "I wanted you to see it before the judge walked by."

I tossed my coat on the hook and joined him at the bay window. "Should I close my eyes?" I asked.

"Then how will you see it?"

"Good point."

The paper ripped away. A marvelously sculpted set of snow loving animals, white birch polar bear, black sunflower seed penguins and an Arctic fox made of white rose petals played in a white carnation snow drift.

"Wow, Ryder, they look so animated." I took a deep breath. "And they smell good. They are perfect. It's perfect." I gave him a quick hug.

"I've got to climb inside and pulled down the paper on the window pane. Go outside and see how it looks from the sidewalk."

"Yes, I can't wait." I headed outside and immediately regretted peeling off my coat so fast. I hugged myself and did a little dance to keep warm as he tore away the paper.

"Well?" he called through the glass.

"It's gorgeous."

"It certainly is," Lester said from behind. "Next time, I'm going to have Ryder decorate my window. Yolanda only spent one minute looking at mine. She's writing some notes on her clipboard." He added an eye roll to that. "And then she's coming to your shop."

Yolanda had enlisted the help of Franki's son. I wasn't sure which one because Tyler and Taylor were so identical, I couldn't tell them apart. Especially when I only saw one. Franki's twin daughters were easier to distinguish because they had different taste in clothing and different hairstyles, but that wasn't the case with her boys. Taylor or Tyler was carrying a small trophy and a blue ribbon.

Yolanda reached my shop window.

"How is everything going, Yolanda?"

She groaned as her shoulders fell. "Things would be a lot better if people didn't keep getting killed during my planned events. I put all this time and effort into making things perfect."

"Yes, I know you do. And you do an incredible job."

"Thank you. But what's the use of turning the town into a story-book Christmas town when a man is just going to end up dead in the middle of it all. Not that I'm blaming him. Poor man." She blew out a frustrated breath. "Anyhow, let's see what you have." She walked up to the window to get a better look. "Oh my goodness, this is adorable. You outdid yourself, Lacey."

"Yes I did. I hired an incredible assistant. Ryder did this all on his own."

My innocent confession caused her mouth to purse together in disapproval. Ryder was watching anxiously through the window to gauge Yolanda's reaction. I showed him a thumbs up to let him know she loved it, even though I was sure my big mouth had just cost him the trophy.

I let Yolanda do her judge thing and stepped back with Lester, who was chatting with Franki's son. Instantly, my sense of smell was over-whelmed with the pungent, menthol smell of sore muscle cream.

"Tyler," I said, happily. "You're Tyler," I repeated.

Lester laughed. "He probably already knows that."

"Yes, of course. I was eating at the diner when you called your mom about your injury at practice. She told you to put on the sports cream. Now I can tell you apart from your brother."

"Never thought of that," Tyler said. "But I'm not sure how much longer I can stand the stuff. It's giving me a headache more than it's helping my pulled muscle."

"I'm still excited that I could tell you two apart this morning."

Yolanda wrote something down on her clipboard. "Come, Tyler. Let's walk over to Elsie's shop."

They hurried on to the next window. Lester walked up next to me. He waved into the window at Ryder.

"Did you get any good vibes from her?" Lester asked.

I kept smiling as I spoke because Ryder was watching. "I think I just blew our chances of winning by being too darn honest. And now I have to tell Ryder."

Lester chuckled. "Yeah, that honesty stuff can sometimes get you in the end. I guess I'll get back to brewing coffee and leave window decorating events to people like my sister."

"Have a good day, Les."

# CHAPTER 22

*I* was glad that I'd at least brought truffles to brighten Ryder's otherwise dismal mood. I had warned him that I'd probably taken us out of the running by letting Yolanda know that I'd had no part in the genius and talent behind our window display. I wanted to make sure Ryder got all the credit. I hadn't expected Yolanda to be quite so petty. But I took a lot of photos of the display and posted them on the shop's website so everyone could see it and so that the memory of the amazing display would still be fresh long after the petals and flowers wilted away.

Elsie had also missed out on the trophy, which hadn't surprised me too much because I'd always noticed a hint of tension between Yolanda and Elsie. I often wondered if it stemmed from them both being filled with non-stop energy. There might just have been a touch of competition between them to see who could out-dynamo the other.

And after the entire drama and angst of the window competition, the person who won was sitting behind her computer at her desk in the back office not even wearing a proud smile.

Lola looked up as I walked in.

"Congratulations on the blue ribbon." I sat on the rustic old farm bench in front of her desk.

"Yeah, I don't know what Yolanda was thinking. All I did was dust off a bunch of old toys and arrange them in the window."

I reached into the crystal candy dish at the front of her desk and took out a peppermint. "Not true. There is something about the toys you chose and the way you positioned them that makes them seem as if they were taken right out of a Victorian Christmas card." As I gushed on about her window, she continued clicking away on her keyboard and staring intently at the screen.

"Why, thank you, Pink, what a nice thing to say," I said in my best imitation of Lola.

Her brown eyes peered over the top of the computer. "Sorry, I was just looking something up."

I unwrapped the peppermint. "Let me guess, Dayton Construction and its illustrious owner?" I popped the mint into my mouth, and as predicted, a sneeze followed. I'd never figured out why peppermint made me sneeze.

"Gesundheit," Lola said absently. "Apparently Dayton Construction is only a couple years old. They are based in a town called Rowley, which is about a hundred miles from here." That piece of information made her slim shoulders sag. I had hoped it wouldn't be the case, but my friend still seemed to be obsessing about Randall Dayton. It made me wish we had never walked into Franki's Diner that day.

"A hundred miles is not exactly a day trip." My rational comment earned a disgruntled snort.

Lola's chair creaked as she sat forward. "Wow, the stuff you find when you're snooping around into someone's life. There's a company called Big Bob Construction that keeps coming up with Dayton Construction. It seems Big Bob was owned by Robert Dayton, Randall's father."

She quickly typed something into the search bar.

"I guess I'll go and leave you to your research. I just wanted to congratulate you on your win."

Before I stood up, she raised her hand to stop me from going. "It says that Bob Dayton lost his contractor's license and his company went bankrupt after he was cited for at least a dozen safety violations."

Her finger reached toward the screen as her eyes darted back and forth. "Oh, that's sad." She sat back with a frown. "It seems the whole fiasco drove Big Bob to suicide."

I got up from the chair. "It sounds like Randall comes with a lot of baggage. Something you are better off without." I wasn't going to play the supportive friend with this guy. I hadn't even bothered to mention to her what Dash had told me after his interview with Dayton. I was relieved he wouldn't be in the area for long. "I'm heading back to my store. Catch you later."

I was just about out of her office when she called to me. "Hey, Pink?"

I turned back. "Yeah?

"What was the name of the man they found strangled on the pier?"

The question surprised and confused me. "Chad Ruxley. Why?"

"That's what I thought." She finally lifted her eyes from the monitor. "It says in one of the articles about Big Bob Construction that a sub-contracted plumber working on one of the Big Bob Construction sites had blown the whistle on the company's safety violations. It was Chad Ruxley."

Sometimes a revelation could nearly sweep you off your feet and not in a good way. What were the odds that Randall Dayton's family had a rough and rocky history with Chad Ruxley. I hurried over to her computer to read the article myself. It was dated April 2012. "Chad Ruxley of Ruxley Plumbing was being praised for speaking up about some egregious safety issues, something that Big Bob had been cited for many times. But instead of cleaning up his act, Dayton continued to break the OSHA rules. Ruxley alerted the contractor's board, and they stripped Dayton of his license. The business folded soon after. A year later, Robert Dayton took his own life with a handgun, leaving behind a wife, Patricia and two sons, Randall and Scott."

Ideas and notions were shooting around in my head like a wild game of darts. Was it possible Detective Briggs was overlooking another potential suspect? I was going to head straight over to his office and tell him what I'd just learned. I was sure he'd be interested to hear.

"I'll talk to you later, Lola, and try not to waste—spend too much time on this man. There are many other fish in the sea."

Lola stared at me over her computer. "You didn't just throw the fish in the sea metaphor at me, did you?"

"We live in a coastal town so it works," I chirruped on the way out.

# CHAPTER 23

*I* swept by my shop to grab my coat and gloves and to let Ryder know I was going on an important errand. Then I race walked to the police station as if there were tiny turbo charged wings on my shoes.

Fingers crossed was often my go to move, but it rarely ever worked for me, especially when I was wearing gloves. But this time I was in luck. Detective Briggs' car was parked out front of the police station. Earlier, I'd been anxious to tell him about the scent match with fresh lumber, but I quickly questioned my conclusions. I hated to give him more superfluous information. What he needed was something cogent, something he could use. And it seemed to me I had it.

Hilda was on the radio giving directions to an officer when I walked into the station. She finished the call and removed the headphones. "Good morning, Lacey. Nice to see you." She stood to see me better over the tall counter. "I'm sure you're here to see, Detective Briggs. I'll just let him know." A sheepish grin appeared. "Did you notice what I hung from the ceiling?"

I dropped my head back and stared up at the cluster of mistletoe taped to the ceiling of the station. "I see it now."

"Thought it would add a festive touch to the place." Poor Hilda tried to spruce up the drab, utilitarian office every holiday, but her added touches only seemed to make the place look even more like a police station. Almost as if the small adornments stood out in stark contrast, highlighting just how cold and uninviting the station was.

Hilda's laugh brought my chin back down to my chest. "I think Officer Chinmoor has been hoping a pretty girl would walk in just so he could give the mistletoe magic a try."

Detective Briggs' door opened. His face seemed to light up when he saw me. (At least that was what I was telling myself.) "Miss Pinkerton, I thought I heard another voice out here. I was just on my way to Chad Ruxley's boat to do another sweep for evidence before his brother has it taken to storage."

"I can go with you, if you need a nose."

"That would be great."

"First though, I have some information I think you might find interesting."

"Sure. Come into my office. I have someone waiting to give me a ride out to the boat, but I have a few minutes." Briggs buzzed me through the metal gate between the counters, and we walked into his office.

He stopped short of circling around to his chair and leaned against the front of his desk. "Would you like to sit?"

"No, that's fine. I think you might be overlooking a person of interest, someone who is in town and who has a past with Chad Ruxley. And an unpleasant one at that."

"Go on." He reached back for a notepad and pen.

"Thursday afternoon, Lola and I were in Franki's having lunch when some men from Dayton Construction walked in. The owner of the company, Randall Dayton, was making eyes at Lola, and he asked her to stay for a piece of pie. Which, she did, of course. But that's another topic. They made plans to take a carriage ride together that night during the light show. According to Lola, they had a wonderful time and even stopped for midnight pancakes at the diner. She hasn't heard from him since, and she's quite distraught about it, but again, another topic."

"It's only been two days," Briggs noted in typical man fashion.

"Yes, well, that's not the point of this conversation, and two days is an eternity after a very successful date. But back to my information. Lola was searching online to see what she could find out about Randall Dayton." I held up my hand to stop the imminent eye roll. Briggs might have been more gentlemanly than most, but he was still a man and they sure did stick together when it came to women.

I forged ahead. "A bit of research brought her to an interesting article about Big Bob's Construction. It was a company owned by Robert Dayton, Randall's dad. In 2012, Chad Ruxley was working on Big Bob's work site and he saw a number of safety violations. He alerted the contractor's board and because it wasn't the first time Bob had been cited, they took away his license. The company went bankrupt and folded soon after, which led Bob Dayton to take his own life."

Briggs looked up from his notepad with wide eyes. "Ruxley is purported to be an honest, stand-up kind of guy. I guess this story confirms that." Briggs sat back and seemed to be absorbing the information. He tapped his pen on the notepad, but stopped it abruptly. "Wait. Did you say he and Lola had a date on Thursday night that went until at least past midnight?"

"Yes. Pancakes at Franki's at midnight." My words trailed off as it dawned on me why he was asking. "They were on their date during the murder."

Briggs nodded. "If Lola can confirm and possibly even Franki, then that's a solid alibi. I don't think I would even have to bring him in for questioning."

My posture deflated. "Darn it. I was sure I had something significant this time."

"It's still important. There would certainly be a good motive. Your father's life ruined to the point that he commits suicide. That would stick in anyone's craw." He walked over to his coat and hat. "I'll keep what you told me in mind. In the meantime, let's go take one last stroll around Chad Ruxley's boat."

# CHAPTER 24

*D*erek, the young man Briggs had paid to motor us out to Chad Ruxley's boat, was in his last year of high school. He was pleased to be able to make a 'wad of cash' this weekend ferrying people out to the boats in his two man fishing boat. The shallow metal boat, with two planks running from side to side for seats, provided us with a wild, bumpy ride as he traversed the waves rolling into shore. Twice, I grabbed hold of Detective Briggs' arm certain that I was going to be popped clear off the plank seat and into the ice cold water. And as pillowy as my winter coat looked, I was sure it wasn't going to keep afloat like a life jacket. In fact, the downy filling would, no doubt, soak up sea water like a sponge.

After my second grab, and after I peeled my gloved hand away from him, Briggs reached for my arm and held it. He pushed up that sideways grin and avoided eye contact.

"Thank you," I said quietly.

"You're welcome."

I was amazed at how much more secure I felt with him holding my arm. I briefly let myself wonder if that same level of security would be there even if I wasn't trying to keep my bottom inside a jolting, bouncing boat.

"We're here," Derek announced, in case we didn't notice the twenty foot sailboat bobbing in the tide just inches from our faces. "Make sure you have all your belongings with you. Wallets, keys, handkerchiefs." He pulled a box out from under the plank he sat on. "I've already got a collection. Bumpy rides tend to make things fall out of pockets. Now I'm reminding people after each ride."

Detective Briggs and I both patted pockets for phones and other belongings. "I think I've got everything," I said as I stood in the boat and then fell back down hard on my bottom. "Except my sense of balance, which I believe I left somewhere back on the beach."

Derek had a good laugh over that.

Detective Briggs stood first and then helped me up. It was quite a feat to stay steady, but Briggs kept a tight grip on me. I moved forward to reach for the ladder hanging off the stern. As my eyes swept past the box of left behind items, a flash of white caught my eye. "This handkerchief," I said as I reached into the box and picked it up.

Detective Briggs lifted it to get a better look. "It's the same handkerchief we saw Charlene Ruxley use at the campsite."

"She told me she hand-stitches them herself and then sells them at events."

Briggs looked at our young captain. "Do you happen to remember who dropped this?"

"I do. A lady. One of the Christmas carolers. In fact, I was taking her out to this same boat, the *Sea Gem*."

"Do you remember when she went to the boat?"

Derek pulled out his phone. "I've got all the appointments on my phone. Charlene Ruxley ten o'clock A.M. on Thursday. She had me hang around so I could ferry her back to shore. She didn't stay long. I heard some angry voices up on the deck. When she climbed back on the boat, she was crying and clutching that handkerchief. We got back to shore, and she nearly jumped out of the boat. I didn't notice she had dropped the handkerchief until she was too far away."

"Thank you," Briggs said. "And if you don't mind sticking around for us, we won't be long. I'll pay you for the time."

Derek saluted. "At you service, Detective Briggs."

With some fortitude and very little grace, I managed to pull myself up the ladder and over the stern of the *Sea Gem*. Briggs climbed aboard and immediately pulled out his notebook to write down what Derek had told him.

I looked around at the deck. "Why do you think Charlene said she hadn't seen her ex-husband in a long time? Seems there was no way her visit to the *Sea Gem* could have slipped her mind. Especially since she left the boat crying."

"Not sure but I'll definitely be making a trip out to their campsite when Derek takes us back to shore. The boat has been given a pretty thorough search, but I thought you could do one trip around to see if anything stands out to you." He held up the handkerchief. "Like this highly important piece of evidence you found."

I gave a satisfied nod and took a stroll around the deck. Again, the clammy weather and the strong smell of the ocean made the task difficult. The holiday decorations were still fluttering in the wind. The sight of them made me sad to think that just two days ago Chad Ruxley, a good man by all accounts, was enjoying himself, decorating his boat and excited to be part of an annual celebration.

I walked down three steps into a tiny cabin area that was set up with a coffee maker and a mini refrigerator. I took deep breaths but didn't pick up anything. Even the coffee maker was dry and nearly free of aroma.

I turned and noticed a small narrow closet on the side of the cabin. I heard Detective Briggs' footsteps coming down the metal stairs as I opened the closet. A broom, a mop and bucket were inside the narrow cabinet along with some cleaning supplies. I breathed in deeply.

"Anything?" Briggs asked over my shoulder.

"Just what I'd expect in a closet full of cleaning supplies. Nothing that reminds me of the chemical smell on his sweater. Which reminds me, in my haste to tell you about the connection with Randall Dayton, I forgot to mention that I was talking to—" I hesitated, not wanting to bring up the one name that could change Briggs' mood instantly. But I'd already started the sentence, and I didn't know how else to finish it. "I was talking to Dash," I said quickly, hoping the name would have less impact. But I caught a glimmer of a flinch on his face. "He was carrying some lumber up to his porch, and it occurred to me that the smell on Chad's sweater and on the ribbon might have been lumber. Douglas Fir, to be exact, because that's the kind of wood he's using on his porch."

A churlish grin crossed his face. "Maybe your neighbor is our suspect." He even avoided using the name in his snide remark. One day, I'd get to the bottom of their mutual dislike for each other. Whatever it was, it was something deep and longstanding.

"Anyhow," I said tersely. "I thought I'd mention it."

"Yes, sorry." He pulled out his notebook and wrote it down. "Well, it seems there is nothing new to discover here. In fact, the ride to the boat might have been more productive. Let's get back to shore. I'm sure you need to get back to your shop, and I need to talk to Charlene Ruxley and find out why she lied."

# CHAPTER 25

wo news vans rolled into town after lunch, and the quiet lull that had been cast over the town after the discovery of a body on the pier had been lifted. People, it seemed, had pushed the tragedy to the back of their minds, and some of the pre-murder enthusiasm for the light show had returned. But something told me the news crews wouldn't be nearly as focused on the holiday flotilla as they would be on Chad Ruxley's unexplained, violent death.

Ryder proved my theory true as he came in from lunch.

"Mayor Price is walking around with his hair on fire," Ryder said as he hung up his coat and beanie.

"I wouldn't mind seeing that." I put the finishing touches on a happy birthday bouquet for a customer pick-up. "Although, it's probably just as well that I was not around because my presence seems to make that fire burn brighter. Why is he so upset?"

Ryder hopped on the stool to finish the soda he'd carried back with him. "I guess the two news crews that are setting up on opposite sides of the beach are asking questions and interviewing people about the murder case. Sort of puts a bad light on a festive celebration. After all, the boats had already gone through several beach towns, only to end here, in Port Danby, with one of the boat owners strangled. Price figures it's very bad publicity for our town."

"He's right about that." I turned the bouquet of pink and yellow roses around to check it out from every angle. "How's this?"

"Looks good. Is that a delivery?"

"No, the customer is coming to pick it up."

The door opened and Lola walked into the shop still looking dreary and downtrodden, a detail Ryder apparently missed.

He clapped loudly. "The window display champion of Harbor Lane. Congratulations. Your window is very cool."

Lola forced a smile. "I'm still confused about how I won. My window doesn't compare to yours or to Elsie's." It was only a half-hearted compliment, but I sensed that coming from Lola it had made Ryder's day. He headed to the potter's table with a spring in his step.

Lola shuffled to the work island and climbed up onto the stool. She propped her elbows onto the island and rested her chin in her hands. Her sullen expression sparked an idea.

"Hey, my friend, how about coming to my house for dinner? I will make a feast of comfort food, foods that have no business being on the same plate together but that as a whole represent all that is good in the world of food. I'm thinking mashed potatoes and gravy, macaroni and cheese and maybe, just to pretend we're trying, some of those green beans that are drowned in cream of mushroom soup and deep fried onions. You know—" I curled my fingers into air quotes. "The *vegetable* dish they serve at Thanksgiving. We'll top the entire calorie binge off with some of Elsie's caramel cake. What do ya say?"

She took a dramatic breath. "I suppose I could work up some enthusiasm for mashed potatoes and macaroni and cheese. Maybe then I'll just drift into a carb coma and wake up Monday, forgetting this weekend even happened."

I was sure the Dayton construction project would last well past this weekend, but I wasn't about to point that out to her. With any luck, Dayton would stay over in Chesterton and not travel to Port Danby at all.

"What time do you want me to drag my sorry bottom to your house?" she asked.

I rested my arms on the counter and looked pointedly at her. "If you're going to *drag* yourself or even your sorry bottom to my house, then stay home and I'll eat mashed potatoes alone. Seriously, Lola, enough. Come over and we'll eat, laugh and watch a movie. And no dragging or sorry bottomness, agreed?"

Lola nodded once. "Agreed." Her eyes and mouth opened wide. "Oh my gosh, I nearly forgot." She glanced at her phone. "Yikes, I'm late." She hopped off the stool.

"Where are you heading?"

"Oddly enough, to the police station. In fact, this whole thing with Randall has me in such a twist, I forgot my main reason for coming in here. Why do you think Detective Briggs wants to see me? He said he just had a few quick questions about Thursday night. I'm baffled."

I knew exactly what the questions were, but it wasn't my place to tell her. "Hmm, not sure. I think he might be asking around to people who were out late on Thursday. And I might have mentioned that you were out on a date that night."

"Really?" She looked even more perplexed. Her face smoothed to concern. "Gosh, I'm not a suspect am I? Just because I was out late?"

"No, silly. You're not a suspect." I reached for my coat. "But I'll walk down there with you. I have a few questions for the detective myself."

# CHAPTER 26

*L*ola stood in front of the tall counter at the police station like a little girl waiting to go in and see the school principal. She fidgeted with the zipper on her coat, lifting it up and down, and twice, getting it jammed on the fabric. I finally placed my hand over hers to stop her from pulling it down again.

Hilda finished a call and twirled her chair. "What are you girls up to today? Did you see the news reporters? They are setting up cameras for the light show, but from what I hear, they are spending more time snooping around, trying to find out nuggets about the homicide case." She sat forward quickly. "Lola, I wanted to ask you about a certain kind of lamp I saw on Ebay. I was wondering if you had one like it in your shop." She began clicking away on her mouse.

Hilda had apparently decided Lola and I had stopped in just to chat. "Hilda, I think Detective Briggs needed to ask Lola some questions."

"Oh, did he?" She waved her hand. "Of course. I should have asked. I'll find that lamp in the meantime. It's a rose cut hurricane lamp that I think would go perfectly with my new sofa." She got sidetracked again with her lighting fixture questions and then stopped herself. "I'm just a scatter brain today. A few new pieces of furniture and my mind is

118

mired in interior decorating ideas. Just a minute." She knocked on the door and poked her head in. "Lola and Lacey are here to see you." She laughed. "Sounds like a song or a music group." She repeated our names in a sing song voice. Her new furniture had definitely put her in a cheerful mood. "Go right in, girls."

"Actually, Lola, you should probably go in first. I'll wait out here. After all, it was you he needed to talk to. I just came along as an afterthought."

Lola nervously reached for her zipper. "Are you sure?"

"You can come in too, Miss Pinkerton." Briggs was at his office door. "I just have a few quick questions for Miss Button. Then I need to talk to you."

Lola twittered nervously as she fidgeted with the zipper. "I haven't been called Miss Button since Mrs. Rushing, the vice principal in high school, called me that when she was mad about something. And she was always mad. But I had to hand it to her, she had everyone's last names memorized. She once called me Miss Button over the loud-speaker. I hadn't done anything wrong, but—" Lola was heading into one of her long, rambling nerve-fueled narratives. I knew I needed to intervene, or we'd all grow old and gray hearing about her high school antics and Mrs. Rushing.

"Lola," I said sharply to get her attention. "Detective Briggs is probably busy."

"Oh, right."

Briggs nodded a silent thanks at me as he buzzed us through to his office. Lola was more relaxed when she realized I was walking into the office with her. She had nothing to be nervous about, of course, but I was sure it was her first time in his office. The way she surveyed the room assured me I was right.

"So, this is what a detective's office looks like," Lola said as she sat in the chair across from his desk. "Oops, I forgot to ask permission to sit."

"Of course you can sit," Briggs said, as he circled around to his chair. I sat in the second chair and wriggled to get comfortable, but the chairs weren't really made for comfort.

Briggs pulled out his notebook, which caused Lola to reach for her zipper pull. I put my hand gently on her arm and shook my head. She lowered her hands to her lap.

Briggs looked up from his notebook. The lighting in his office was that horrid fluorescent department store dressing room type that highlighted every dimple of fat while you slithered into tight jeans. But James Briggs, I'd discovered, looked good under any light. The case he'd been working on was making him look more weary than usual, but he was still handsome sitting behind his desk.

"I'm sure Miss Pinkerton filled you in on why I asked you here."

"No, I didn't," I admitted quickly. I could feel Lola's questioning gaze on the side of my face, and suddenly, I, too, had an urge to fiddle with my zipper pull. "I'm sorry, Detective Briggs, but I only just found out that you called her here." I tried to shoot him a 'what on earth' look, but it was hard with Lola just twelve inches away, boring a hole in the side of my face with her puzzled scowl. "I, uh, didn't think it was my place."

It finally dawned on Briggs that he shouldn't have tossed me into the mix. He cleared his throat, as if that might erase his missteps. Unfortunately, there was no delete or backspace button for spoken words. (Someone really should come up with that.)

"I apologize. That was presumptuous of me," Briggs said. "Miss Button, as you know, a man was murdered on the pier. It took place on Thursday night around eleven o'clock. It has come to my attention that a construction company is working on a home site in Beacon Cliffs. The owner of that company, Randall Dayton, has some unpleasant history with the victim, Chad Ruxley."

Lola lifted a brow my direction. "It came to your attention, did it?" Lola had figured out why she was there. "I had a date with Randall Dayton on Thursday night."

Briggs wrote down a note. "What time did the date start and when did it end?"

Lola's eyes rolled up as if she had to give it some thought, which I knew was baloney because she had thought of little else except that date since Thursday. "Let's see. I met him at the carriage stop on

Pickford Way at nine. He was about five minutes late. Then we took two rides. At nine-thirty we walked along the beach to look at the lights. Around ten o'clock, we took a stroll around the town square and along Culpepper Road just to talk and get to know each other. And there was one—" Lola paused and a pink blush rose in her cheeks.

Briggs lifted his gaze from his notes and seemed to figure out that the next word was kiss. He cleared his throat again. "Right. What happened after the walk?"

"We decided to go to Franki's and have pancakes. Franki wasn't there, of course, but Terrence, the night manager served us. I'm sure he'll remember."

Briggs finished writing. "That's all I need from you, Miss Button. Thank you for taking the time to come down here. Miss Pinkerton, if you have a few extra minutes, I have some information about the handkerchief."

"No problem."

Lola stood up. "I guess I'll head back to the store then."

"Is seven o'clock good for dinner?" I asked her before she walked away.

"I'll be there with my stretch waist mashed potato eating pants on," Lola said. "See you then."

"Mashed potato eating pants?" Briggs asked.

"You don't have a pair?" I scooted forward. "What happened with the handkerchief? Did you talk to Charlene Ruxley?"

"I did." He flipped back through his notebook. "She admitted that she did go see her ex-husband on the day of his murder. She said she had a highly personal matter to discuss with him, and she left there upset because he reacted very badly to their conversation. She wasn't being interrogated, so I couldn't pry further into the highly personal matter. But I will bring her in for a formal interview if necessary. Charlene did mention that she left him because she just wasn't in love with him. Chad was pretty broken up about it."

"Why did she lie about it when we talked to her at the campsite?"

"She was sure it would implicate her in the murder. To which I pointed out that the lying to avoid implication had moved her up on my person of interest list."

"How did she respond to that?"

"She cried. Fortunately, that woman seems to have an endless supply of those fancy handkerchiefs. Unfortunately, I don't feel like I'm any further along on this case. Anything come to you on the scents on the victim's sweater and the murder ribbon?"

"A murder ribbon. That could almost be classified as an oxymoron like pretty ugly and clearly confused. I actually walked down here with Lola to ask if I could have one more go at the sweater and ribbon. Are they still here or have you sent them off?"

"We only sent off small samples of each for the time being." Briggs stood up. "Follow me. It's a good idea for you to smell them again. Maybe the scent will be stronger inside the evidence room than outside on a cold pier soaked with fish odor."

I followed him down the short hallway. The evidence room was very 'small town', and it made me smile. There were two metal tables and a tall file cabinet. Briggs walked to a cabinet and unlocked it. He pulled out a large baggie with the sweater and a smaller baggie with the ribbon. He pulled out latex gloves from a box on top of the file cabinet and pulled them on.

He unzipped the baggies and laid the sweater on the table. I leaned down over the garment. I could still smell the onions from Chad Ruxley's last meal and the woodsy smell was there too. It was concentrated mostly around the neck of the sweater and the ribbon.

"It's definitely easier to discern the smells in this room. And I'm standing by the smell of lumber, like the Douglas Fir Dash was carrying onto his porch." I looked up at him. "And no, he's not your suspect. But, that reminds me—" I paused. "This has to do with Dash. Do you think you can handle me bringing up his name several times or should I relay this to Officer Chinmoor?"

His jaw twitched, showing he was irritated with me, but he knew I was right.

"No, Miss Pinkerton, I think I can handle it."

"Dash needs some extra work while the boat servicing business is slow. He interviewed with Randall Dayton for the Beacon Cliffs construction job. I believe he was offered the position, but he turned it down."

Briggs couldn't hold back a scoff. "Figures," he grumbled.

I tilted my head to make sure he was done with his side notes.

"Sorry, go ahead. Why did he turn it down?"

I thought back to the reasons Dash gave and suddenly wished I had something more concrete. "Dash said there was something about Dayton that he didn't like. He realized he didn't want to work for him."

I predicted the blank expression that followed, and I was silently kicking myself for bringing it up at all.

"I just wrote down Lola's statement that provides a solid alibi for Randall Dayton. And I don't think I can bring him in for questioning just because Vanhouten had *a feeling*."

"Argh, I knew I shouldn't have brought up his name or anything he said. I just thought it provided some character detail for a person of interest."

"Which, at this point, he's not." I hated when he talked in a curt, succinct manner.

There was a chilled silence in the room as he took the ribbon out from the bag. I leaned down to smell it. "It's a chemical smell, but I just don't know what it is. It's nothing I've ever smelled before."

Briggs pushed the evidence back into the baggies. "Miss Pinkerton, the history you brought up about Dayton's father and Chad Ruxley is important. I shouldn't have brushed it off so fast."

I didn't know how to respond. And I didn't really want to at the moment.

"While he seems to have a sound alibi, I'm going to head out to the site and talk to him. Can't hurt to ask him a few questions about his history with Ruxley."

"Do what you think is right. You're the detective." I was having a hard time getting past the hurt I was feeling.

The same chilly silence followed us out of the evidence room. He stopped by the hook in his office to grab his coat before walking me out.

"Hilda, I've got some more people to interview. I'll be back in a few hours."

I pushed out the gate and felt him right behind me.

"Miss Pinkerton."

I kept walking.

"Lacey, I'm sorry."

I stopped but didn't turn around. I wasn't sure I wanted to look at him.

"Oh my!" Hilda said, excitedly, causing me to turn around anyhow.

Briggs was standing just a foot away, looking way too appealing with his apologetic brown eyes.

"Look up," Hilda said. "Look where you two landed."

My eyes lifted up to the cluster of mistletoe. Briggs and I gazed at each other for a long moment. It seemed there was a small hurricane of emotions swirling through the air. I would be lying to myself if I thought that the idea of kissing Detective Briggs had never crossed my mind. But I was still feeling the sting of the last few minutes. Then there was the audience of one, a very anxious looking Hilda watching and waiting. Mistletoe or not, there was nothing right about the moment for a kiss.

"Good day, Detective Briggs."

"Good day, Miss Pinkerton," he said quietly.

# CHAPTER 27

*I* left the police station thinking I'd come up with the comfort food dinner idea to brighten Lola's mood, only now I needed a little brightening myself. It was technically my fault for bringing up Dash, but I refused to feel bad for it. When the notion popped into my head, I thought it might add another layer of dimension to Randall Dayton's character. But I kept forgetting that he had an alibi that took him off the suspect list.

I needed some potatoes and cheese for our carbohydrate overload party and decided to stop in at the Corner Market before heading back to the shop. Gigi and Tom Upton, the owners of the Corner Market, had decorated their picturesque, brightly painted shop with white icicle lights. A whimsical snowman scene had been hand painted on the front window. I always marveled at just how many goods they carried in their store. It was no bigger than my flower shop, but their incredible sense of organization and their quest to use every available inch of space had allowed them to stock everything from produce and toiletries to seasonal decorations. The front two tables in the center of the store were overflowing with perfect items for a great gift basket—cheeses, sausages, special syrups and hot sauces in small bottles.

Molly and Buddy, the Upton's dachshunds were decked out in matching green sweaters. Molly wagged her tail and greeted me as I walked past the counter.

A deep, unfamiliar voice rounded the snack food shelves. I didn't catch the words but since a feminine laugh followed, I could only assume it was something comical. I walked around the potato chip stand and had to work hard not to appear stunned. Randall Dayton, still dressed in work clothes and the yellow Dayton hat, was staring into the drink refrigerator with a blonde woman who was wearing slick black pants and a pair of ankle boots that were trimmed in fur. I'd never seen the woman before but then there were a lot of people in town for the flotilla. He glanced up briefly and seemed to recognize me, although we had only passed each other once in the diner just before the pie date.

I smiled politely and squeaked past them to the cheese section. I took a quick sniff as I passed by, but the only scent in the air was perfume. Not an expensive one but not a cheap one either, I quickly assessed before turning off my perfumer's nose. One thing I didn't smell was cigarette smoke. If Randall was a smoker like Lola had complained, then he washed well before work and he made sure not to light up on the job. It would also mean that he never smoked in his work truck because the stench of tobacco lingered on everything, even car seats.

They made their drink choices and walked up to the counter. I was incredibly relieved that Lola had gone back to the antique shop earlier. She would have been terribly distraught to see that the bum had already moved on. Maybe he figured his time was limited in town and he might as well make the best of it.

Gigi finished ringing them up. They walked out as I carried my block of cheddar and russet potatoes to the counter.

Gigi shook her head. "That man sure gets around."

"Who? The man with the yellow hat?"

"Yes."

"How so?" Tom and Gigi's market was right at the corner of Harbor Lane and Pickford Way, an intersection of the two most well-traveled streets in town. Everyone, both locals and tourists, frequented their market. The market's position gave them a portal into just about everything happening in town.

"He was in here just an hour earlier with—" Gigi paused and seemed to consider whether or not to divulge the name. I could only assume it was someone local.

"That's all right, Gigi. I understand."

Gigi smiled weakly. She leaned closer and lowered her voice. "Tom doesn't like it when I gossip. So many people walk through this shop that we see it all."

"That's because it's a wonderful shop."

Gigi beamed at the compliment. "Thank you." She rang me up and handed me the bag with my cheese and potatoes.

"Are you making scalloped potatoes or baked potatoes topped with butter and cheese?" she asked.

"Hmm, no, but something along those lines."

Gigi closed the register. "You can't go wrong with potatoes and cheese."

"You are so right. I'll see you later, Gigi." I leaned down and pet both dogs. "And I'll see you two later too."

"Are you going to watch the lights again tonight?" Gigi asked. "It's been bustling around here today with the news crews in town."

"I'll bet. Not sure if I'm going to be there or not. Say hi to Tom for me." I walked out of the store and was just about to turn north to head back to the shop when something caught my eye across the street.

Not wanting to be seen, I slipped around to stand on the far side of the market. The couple leaving Franki's Diner together knew that I was working with Detective Briggs on the murder case. I watched as Tim Ruxley and Charlene walked across the street and toward the pier. It was perfectly logical that two people who knew each other and who had mutually lost someone recently might meet for a meal. Just as it was perfectly logical for me to follow them. I was, after all, working on the case.

# CHAPTER 28

*W*ith the news crews and boat owners getting ready for the evening light show, it was a simple task to follow Tim and Charlene unnoticed. I even managed to lose sight of them, once or twice, as they walked through the maze of activity on the pier. Charlene was wearing a bright blue wool coat and ivory white scarf, which made her easier to spot in the crowd than Tim Ruxley in his dark gray coat and black pants.

I thought I was directly behind them and that they were heading straight to the beach, when the flash of bright blue wool caught my eye. I stepped around one of the decorated pylons to see what had made them take a sharp left turn. Charlene and her brilliant blue coat were standing in front of a trestle style table that had been set up just past the seafood stand. I had to lean side to side to get a good glimpse of the table and the people around it. I instantly recognized Jonah and Kendra, two of the carolers. The other pair of singers had joined them as well. Adjacent to the table, they had set up a sign listing items for purchase. Along with their music CDs, they were selling candles, bells and embroidered handkerchiefs. It seemed someone had recently built the trestle table. I wasn't an expert on wood, but the table seemed to have the same hue and natural markings as the Douglas Fir lumber on Dash's new porch. Could that table have been the source of the woodsy smell on Chad's sweater?

As I pondered that possibility, the targets of my mission had continued on toward the beach. If the two had just stopped to have a meal and talk about old times or quite possibly Chad's burial arrangements, then it seemed odd that Charlene would have walked past her group to leave with her ex-brother-in-law.

I shoved my bag of food under my arm and pulled off my gloves as I scooted through the people milling about the pier. I managed to make it to the table where the caroling group was selling their wares.

Kendra was placing bells on the table. She recognized me right away. She was not in costume yet, and she wore a green knitted cap and matching scarf over a dark blue puffy parka. "Miss Pinkerton, right?"

"Yes. I see you have all your goods out for sale." I placed my free hand casually on the table as I browsed the candles and bells. "I'll have to remember to bring my wallet tonight."

"We'll be singing right here, in view of the cameras and reporters." She placed her hand aside her mouth in an attempt to speak privately. "It never hurts to have publicity. It gets us a lot more singing jobs."

"I would think so. And with your wonderful costumes and terrific voices, I'm sure you'll have too many job offers to fill." I looked around. "Where's Charlene, uh—" I snapped my fingers and realized that they were already too cold to get a good sound. "I know she wanted to be called by her maiden name."

"Carlton. Yes, she does . . . for now." Kendra's apple shaped cheeks were pink from the cold. I wasn't sure what her cryptic comment meant, but it was something that made her smile. "She's off somewhere," she added. "We're technically not open for business yet, but be sure to come by the table tonight."

"I'll do that." My hand brushed over the table. "I might just buy this nice trestle table," I laughed. "It would go beautifully on my patio."

"Isn't it wonderful? Jonah builds them himself. When he's not dressed in Victorian top hats and bellowing out holiday tunes, he's building furniture. In fact . . ." She leaned forward and back searching through the people for Jonah, who had wandered away before I reached the table. "I don't see him, but I'll tell him to bring along some of his business cards tonight."

"Perfect. Thanks."

Kendra motioned to my bare hand. "You should get yourself some gloves. Your hands must be freezing."

"Yes, I have some at my shop. I'll see you tonight."

I walked toward Pickford Beach, hoping that Tim and Charlene hadn't gotten too far. I hadn't expected a lengthy conversation with Kendra to throw me off their scent, metaphorically speaking. And that thought reminded me of the wood scent. I lifted my hand to my face as I hurried down the steps to the sand. It was not easy to smell anything with the salty mist hovering over the beach, but there was a faint smell of wood. Douglas Fir, the same wood I'd smelled on the sweater and ribbon.

I struggled to hold onto my potatoes and cheese while pulling gloves onto my freezing cold fingers. There were plenty of people shuffling around the sand, waiting and watching as the news crews set up equipment. I scanned the beach for the bright blue coat but couldn't find it. As I swung back around to see if they had returned to the pier, the blue fabric flashed brightly against the gray mist.

Tim Ruxley was helping Charlene Ruxley into his inflatable boat. She laughed about something and lost her balance, making me feel a little better about my own lack of grace getting in and out of the thing. She sat down at the back of the boat. Ruxley pushed off and climbed inside.

Thin streams of smoke snaked up from the motor and got lost in the mist. But before they headed out to sea, Tim put his arm around her shoulders. Surprisingly, she turned to face him for a kiss. And it wasn't an in-law kind of kiss. It was a true blue, you-are-the-one kind of kiss.

I hurried back through the crowd and up along the pier. I needed to get back to the shop, but first, I would stop by the police station just to drop this nugget of information in Detective Briggs' lap. I was still miffed at the man, but it seemed as if I'd discovered some things that were important to his case. He was just lucky I didn't hold a grudge for long. (Unlike James Briggs and Dashwood Vanhouten.)

# CHAPTER 29

*H*ilda peered up over the counter as I walked into the station. I glanced up at the mistletoe and walked a wide circle around it to the counter.

"You're back," Hilda said. "Did you run into Detective Briggs on your way?"

"No, actually I came by way of Pickford Beach. So he's not in his office? I have a few things to tell him."

Hilda stood. She was wearing a coy smile. "To be honest, and don't tell him I told you this, he said he was going to the Coffee Hutch to get a hot coffee. But I think he was hoping to see you."

"Was he? About what?"

Her round shoulders came up closer to her ears. "I might be stuck behind a ridiculously tall counter talking through headphones, but I was once a darn good police woman. I can sense things like tension in the air that's thicker than that block of cheddar in your bag. And I think I only added to the tension by pointing out the mistletoe. I apologize for that. I was only having some fun, and since it seems like you two—" She stopped . . . thankfully. "Anyhow, I think Detective Briggs was feeling a little out of sorts about the whole thing. I think that's why he decided to buy some coffee. I imagine he was planning to stop in and see you too."

"Hilda, I'm afraid you're reading way too much into it all. We just had a little disagreement about some evidence. There is no need for you to apologize about the mistletoe, and I'm sorry if we both acted like grumpy Scrooges after you pointed it out. After all, you were just getting in the spirit of the season."

"No, no, I was being a busy body. Anyhow, I think if you head back to your flower shop, you'll meet up with Detective Briggs somewhere along the way."

"Thanks, Hilda. I'll keep a lookout for him."

I walked back to the sidewalk and headed toward Pink's Flowers. I spotted Briggs sipping his coffee as he walked into my shop. I was going to put the unpleasantness behind me. There was a case to solve, and I was sure this time I had something significant to report. On my walk back to Harbor Lane, a few notions had coasted through my head. Was it possible that the highly personal conversation Charlene had with her ex-husband had to do with her relationship with his brother, Tim? How long had they been seeing each other? Had their affair been the real reason she left Chad?

I reached the door. Both Ryder and Briggs turned away from their conversation as I walked inside. I could immediately sense Detective Briggs' apologetic mood.

"Miss Pinkerton," he said quickly and walked toward me. I put the cheese and potatoes on the island and went about the business of removing my coat, hat and gloves.

"I went looking for you at the station," I said before he could continue. "Hilda said you were buying a coffee."

He lifted his cup. "Yes. I needed something hot. Can't seem to warm my bones today. And I wanted to see you as well." He glanced across the shop to Ryder, who was stacking the shelves with new vases. He lowered his voice. "I owe you an apology for earlier. You were trying to impart some information to me, and I was—well, I was—"

"Not receptive?"

"At the very least. I'm sorry."

"Apology accepted." I picked up my cheese. "I need to put this in the flower refrigerator. It's probably all right since the weather outside is basically like refrigeration, but—" I motioned for him to follow. "My earlier information didn't take the investigation very far, but I did find out something rather remarkable on my way out of the Corner Market."

Briggs held the door while I placed the block of cheese on the shelf between the red and the yellow roses. I closed the door and turned to him. "It seems that Charlene and Timothy Ruxley are an item."

"An item? You mean a couple?"

"Exactly. I saw them walking out of Franki's Diner together. I thought that seemed plausible, given their connection and all. But I decided to follow them."

"Naturally," he quipped.

"They walked all the way to Pickford Beach, which reminds me." I lifted my hand to his face. He stared at it in confusion. "Do you smell any wood on there? Douglas Fir, to be exact."

He lowered his nose to my palm. "No."

"I guess that makes sense. It's a very faint scent. When Tim and Charlene were making their way across the pier to their rendezvous on Tim's boat, the caroling group was setting up a table of goods and music CDs to sell tonight. The table was a newly built trestle table, crafted by Jonah, the unfriendly man we met at the campsite. And it was made with Douglas Fir, just like the wood on—" I stopped short of mentioning the porch, deciding we'd already circled that topic once too often.

Briggs pulled out his notebook and started writing. "What about the rendezvous?"

"I didn't stay long on the beach, but as they boated out to the *Cloud Nine*, they kissed."

Briggs looked up, apparently waiting for a little more detail.

"A kiss kiss. The kind you might get if you were standing under the mistletoe with a person you really, really liked."

The man would never turn red or show any strands of being flustered. He was far too calm and cool for that, but I was sure I saw the tell-tale twitch in his jaw, letting me know my words had affected him.

He wrote something down. I briefly wondered if he'd written down exactly what I said or if he'd transcribed it into police language. Then I briefly wondered just what that would be in regards to a kiss.

"I think Charlene went out to Chad's boat to let him know that she was with Tim, maybe even engaged to him and Chad got upset."

"That would also explain the argument you witnessed between the two brothers," he added.

"Exactly my thoughts."

"But why kill him?" Briggs asked. "There still isn't an obvious motive."

"I'm not sure." We walked back to the front of the shop. "You're right. If anything, if Chad Ruxley still had feelings for Charlene, then he would be the likely suspect and his brother Tim would be in cold storage at the morgue. Darn, and I thought I had something significant to give you."

"You did. A connection between Tim and Charlene adds another layer to the mystery and to the family relationship. Especially since neither of them mentioned it when I interviewed them. I just need to do some digging to find out what other secrets they have." He took another drink of coffee. "I'll let you get back to work. I think I need to make another trip out to the *Cloud Nine* to talk to Tim Ruxley."

# CHAPTER 30

ingston insisted on trying the noodles I'd cooked for the macaroni and cheese. He mostly played with the wet noodles and even got one stuck on the end of his talon, but he finished every last bit before I covered his cage for the night. Nevermore, on the other hand, was more interested in the sliver of grated cheese that had fallen to the floor as I dropped it into the thick, bubbling roux.

Lola knocked on the door. I gave the cheese sauce one last stir to mix in the cheese and pulled it off the flames to keep it from burning before hurrying to the door.

Lola held up a DVD in each hand, both were Pride and Prejudice. She stepped inside. "We've got two choices. Colin Firth, with his expressive black eye brows, posh accent and the infamous pond swim and wet shirt scene." She held up the second DVD. "Or, Mathew Macfadyen with his blue eyes, envious eyelashes and the infamous standing in the rain and nearly kissing scene."

"I'm good with either. They all end up with Elizabeth gloriously happy and the mistress of a marvelously big estate."

"Let's do Macfadyen. It's much shorter, and I have a feeling after loading up on carbs, I'm not going to be able to keep my eyes open for long."

"I thought we were going to walk down to the beach for the final light display. I told Elsie we'd walk by and pick her up at nine. I could text her and tell her we're skipping it."

"No, that's all right. We can go." Lola plodded to the couch and placed the movies on the coffee table. "With any luck, I'll run into you-know-who. Then I can give him a piece of my mind."

I'd decided almost immediately after seeing Randall with another woman, and especially after the tidbit of gossip Gigi threw my way, that I wouldn't mention the incident to Lola. I was sticking to that plan. With any luck, we would not cross paths with him tonight.

"Lola, the best thing to do would be to ignore him and pretend you don't even know who he is. If you confront him, he'll know he left an impact on you. And for men like that, it's best to let them think they were a mere blip in your life, so small and insignificant you never gave him another thought." I spoke fast to get out my thoughts before she stopped me with her own counterargument. But it turned out I didn't have to prattle on so quickly.

Lola hugged me. "You are wise beyond your years, my friend. And you are right." She walked past me. "I smell cheese sauce and Elsie's caramel cake."

"Yep, let me mix together the noodles and cheese and double check on the potatoes I've got boiling on the stove. Then I thought we could sip some hot tea and watch the lights from my porch while the casserole bakes."

"Sounds good to me. Especially since your neighbor, who is nicer to look at than any decorated boats, was working on his porch when I drove up."

I shook my head, even though nothing Lola said ever surprised me. I stuck a fork into a potato but it didn't come out quickly. I set the timer on my phone for five minutes. I stirred together the macaroni and cheese sauce and put it in the oven while Lola got the tea ready.

We didn't bother with coats, but we pulled on our scarves and beanies. Steaming tea cups in hand, we sat on the top step. The night was mostly clear, save for a few pillowy clouds that took turns drifting past the half moon. The tea tasted especially comforting with the glacial air spinning around our cheeks and noses. We couldn't see Dash's porch from where we sat, but we could hear him sanding wood.

"With all that's been going on," I said in between sips, "I forgot to tell you, I went out to Chesterton to look at old newspaper articles about the Hawksworth murders."

Lola pulled her beanie down lower on her head to keep out the cold. "Why?"

"I told you, I find the whole thing intriguing and mysterious."

"What's so mysterious about a man killing his family and himself in a fit of jealousy?"

My breath puffed out into the cold night air. "That's just it. I don't think Bertram was the killer. I think he was a victim, along with the rest of his family." I was about to continue on when I saw that Lola's attention had been diverted by my handsome neighbor. I silently asked myself just how we became friends when we had so little in common.

Dash waved to us. Lola elbowed me. "He's waving at you, Pink."

"He's waving at both of us." I waved back.

He picked up several pieces of lumber and then tromped back across his lawn, splashing through a sizeable puddle on his way back to the porch. The water seemed to just roll off his work boots.

"Hmm, waterproofing," I said thinking aloud like always. "I've been meaning to get that stuff to spray on my shoes."

"I have some at the shop. But I suggest you spray it outside. It smells kind of strong."

An alibi provided by none other than my friend, Lola, had taken Randall Dayton off the person of interest list, but my mind kept jumping back to him. Of all the people in the vicinity, Randall was the one with a clear cut motive. Chad Ruxley had caused him and his family a great deal of grief. The first time we had seen Randall, one of his crew members had chided him for not waterproofing his new work boots. When we saw him at the work site, he went right through a puddle, without a second thought. That seemed to indicate that at some point between the diner and the day we saw him at the construction trailer, he had sprayed his work boots.

I hopped up so fast, Lola spilled her tea. "Are your potatoes ready?" she asked.

"Soon. I just need to walk over and ask Dash something. Why don't you go inside and turn off the stove. I'll be right in to whip up the mashed potatoes."

"I see, a little private time with the dreamy neighbor."

I stopped at the bottom step and looked up at her. "Seriously, we need to find you a hobby or something to take your mind off men."

Lola stood up. "I think that's where mashed potatoes and caramel cake come in. And hurry back. I'm hungry."

"I'll be right there." I walked over to Dash's house.

He was just cleaning up his tools for the night. He heard me approach and spun around. "I apologize if I was too loud. I'm done for the night."

"No problem. Are you going down to the marina to watch the lights?"

"Nah, I'm meeting some friends in Mayfield."

"I won't keep you then. I just wanted to ask you about your boots."

He rocked his feet up and stared down at them. "I don't know if you'll like them. They are kind of heavy for scooting around a flower shop."

"Very funny. I noticed they aren't getting wet out here in the mosaic of puddles on your lawn. Did you spray them with something to make them waterproof?"

"Yes, I think it's called Water Guard. I have it right here with my tools. You can borrow it if you like. Spray it outside though. It's kind of strong."

"That's what I've heard. Do you mind if I spray a little into the air. I'd like to see what it smells like."

He stared at me in confusion. "You want to smell it?"

"It's for the case I'm working on with—" I stopped short of saying the name that I knew always put Dash in a darker mood. I sighed in frustration. It was terribly hard to know both men and not be able to make mention of the other in front of them. "It has to do with the murder case."

Dash disappeared behind a stack of wood and emerged with a green and white can. He shook it up and took off the lid. He squirted some of the mist into the air. I didn't need to take a deep breath or move closer to get a good whiff of it. It was certainly as strong as Lola and Dash had warned.

"The smell wears off once it's dry," Dash noted.

"That's good to know. Unfortunately, it's not the odor I was looking for. But thanks for your time. Have fun with your friends."

"Thanks. You too."

I headed back to my house. I was having no luck trying to chase down that chemical smell. I didn't even know if it would be helpful. It really felt like this murder case was taking me in circles.

# CHAPTER 31

$\mathcal{A}$fter filling ourselves with the starchiest meal in the history of meals, Lola and I had two choices. Either plunk down on the couch like sacks of potatoes and stare absently at a blue-eyed version of Mr. Darcy or walk down to Elsie's and to the town to try and regain our dignity by burning off the overload of calories. After some heavy-duty mind debates, we opted for the walk. It was a little too early in the evening to slip into a carbohydrate stupor.

Lola zipped up her coat and stared down at herself. "I could swear it's tighter than when I first walked in here tonight. Do you think I already gained weight from that dinner?"

"Only if your body can digest and absorb an entire meal just a half hour after it was consumed." I wrapped my scarf around my neck and positioned it so I could pull it up to cover my nose and mouth on the walk down Myrtle Place.

"Must you always be so scientific?" Lola asked.

"Well, I do have a science degree. And you asked." We stepped outside and a blast of cold air made us both scrunch up in our coats.

We headed down to the sidewalk. "Yes, but I expected the usual baloney filled good friend response of 'oh you, Lola, you always look as thin as a runway model. Even in that big clownish parka, even after eating ten thousand calories of potatoes and noodles'."

"I could still tell you that, but it might sound insincere now. And would you really ever want to be as thin as those runway models? They look like they could slip down a crack in the sidewalk and never be seen again. And that's after the camera adds the supposed ten pounds."

"True. They are bizarrely thin." We hurried our pace to Elsie's trying to avoid the biting cold breeze rushing along Myrtle Place. "We are still having that caramel cake later, right? Can't believe we were both too full for cake. Usually my special dessert stomach allows me to eat sweets no matter how stuffed my regular food stomach is."

I laughed. "As your scientific friend, I will point out that animals with multiple stomachs usually spend their day grazing in fields and chewing cud. And, I'm fairly certain, they rarely eat dessert."

"What a waste of extra stomach."

We had a good laugh. I was glad that my plan to get Lola's mind off Randall had worked. She hadn't mentioned him all night, and I felt confident that the Dayton crisis had almost passed.

We turned the corner to Elsie's. We had texted her before leaving my house, and she was already waiting for us on the porch.

"No Lester?" I asked as Elsie met us on the sidewalk. "I thought he might join us."

"He says the cold makes his bones hurt. Besides, his plumber friend is helping him put a drain in for the new bath tub."

"We should buy him a big basket of bath salts and bubbles and sponges for his luxury bathroom," I said as we reached Harbor Lane.

"I think that's a great idea," Elsie said. I had brought it up as a joke, but apparently she was serious. And she knew her brother better than anyone.

"Fun. I think I have just the basket in my shop," Lola added.

There was a line of people waiting by the Mod Frock for a ride in the horse carriage. The clamor of voices and music wafting up from the coast indicated that there was a large crowd of people gathered for the flotilla. It seemed, for now, people had put the unpleasantness of an unsolved murder behind them to finish off what was meant to be a festive weekend.

Elsie and Lola were drawn toward the beach and the display of lights. At first the plan was to have the *Sea Gem* towed away from the other boats to be taken back to Ruxley's marina slip near his home town. But I'd heard through Ryder and a few other people that they had decided to move the boat in between the other boats. Some of the other boat owners had made a large wreath of lights. That was all that was lit on the *Sea Gem* as a tribute to its owner. It was obvious the other boat owners thought highly of Chad Ruxley. That reality made it much harder to think that someone out there hated him enough to knock him on the head and strangle him with holiday ribbon.

"Elsie and I are going to brave the cold wind and go down on the sand to see if we recognize any of the reporters," Lola said.

"You go ahead. I'm going to check out the items for sale on the carolers' table." I wasn't exactly sure what I was looking for at the table, but I hoped something new and significant would jump out at me. I still needed to figure out what the chemical odor was on the sweater and the ribbon. With any luck, I'd find something that matched it.

My best laid plans were delayed by the large group of people standing around the trestle table. I should have predicted that it would be a popular spot on the pier. I decided to let the line shrink some and headed over to the bike rental kiosk where Yolanda and some of the high school kids were selling hot chocolate to raise money for the sports teams. The line there was long too, but I decided to give it a try.

I searched around hoping to see Detective Briggs, but he was not a fan of crowded town events. I wondered if he had gotten any further on the investigation. I was highly curious to know what he'd found out from Tim Ruxley about his relationship with Charlene.

My fortitude paid off, and I reached the front of the cocoa line. One of Franki's sons was filling the cups for Yolanda.

"Hey, Miss Pinkerton," Taylor or Tyler said as he placed the lid on the cup.

I leaned forward and took a deep smell. I had to concentrate to block out the rich fragrance of the cocoa. "Taylor, right?"

He smiled, seemingly thrilled that someone had actually guessed right. "You're getting good at telling us apart. That's pretty fast compared to most people."

"Thanks but I sort of cheated. I saw Tyler this morning when he was helping with the window awards. I know he's been wearing that sharp smelling sports medicine."

"Oh wow, I hadn't thought of that. Maybe I should tell him to wear it all the time. Only he'll have to sleep in the garage because no one can stand to sit or eat or sleep near him."

"Yeah, that might be sort of inconvenient for the family. I'll just have to find something else to help me tell you two apart."

"That's easy." He pointed at his chest with his thumb. "I'm the handsome one."

I laughed at his comment as I handed Yolanda my two dollars. "Looks like things are going pretty well considering," I commented as she handed me my cup.

"Yes, I suppose it could be worse," Yolanda said. "Although someone did die, so maybe not."

The line behind me was getting longer. I nodded my thank you and turned around to scoot off with my hot drink. I was sure it wouldn't be as good as Lester's, but it would be hot and that was all I needed.

I had my head down, trying to keep it out of the bitter cold and keep my face closer to the warmth radiating from the cup, when I heard Kate Yardley's voice. I peered up from my drink.

Kate was decked out in an adorable red coat with white fur trim. Her boots, gloves and hat were all made from shiny black leather. But it wasn't the fashionable holiday attire that had my attention as much as the man she was attached to. Her shiny black gloved hand was wrapped around the arm of Randall Dayton. He had left behind the yellow construction hat and switched out his work clothes for a thick winter coat and beanie.

Gigi was right. The man really got around. And I now knew how to fill in the blank Gigi had left when she talked about Dayton in the store. I wondered when Kate had met him. Even more so, I wondered how on earth the guy had so much spare time to meet and date women when he was running a large construction job.

Kate spotted me, and I was certain she wanted to make sure I saw her. She guided Dayton so that they passed directly in front of me. She didn't bother to say hello, which I pretty much expected. She was probably hoping I'd mention seeing her to Dash. But she could just keep hoping on that. Her date with Randall didn't interest me at all, especially because they seemed to be leaving and walking away from the activity and my heartsick friend, Lola.

They were well past when something struck me. Randall had left the smell of tobacco in his wake. It was strong too, as if he'd just recently smoked a cigarette. Was it possible that he only smoked away from the job site and only when he was out of his work clothes? The whole thing was more than a tad baffling.

# CHAPTER 32

*E*ven though I knew Detective Briggs was still stuck deep in the middle of the murder case, I was relieved that the holiday event was over. Most of the boats had taken down their decorations and some were already making their way back up the coast. A lot of tourists were still lingering in town, but most would be gone by afternoon. I looked forward to the return of some quiet in Port Danby.

Miraculously, Lola, Elsie and I had managed to get through the rest of the evening without any drama, which by drama I meant running into a certain construction worker and his busy dating agenda. Seeing Dayton with Kate Upton on his arm would have erased all the good the comfort food and caramel cake feast had done. In fact, Lola seemed to be back on her way to her usual good spirits. I only wished that Dayton Construction had been packing up along with the boat owners. I knew little about building houses, but I was sure they'd be around for at least a few more months.

I headed to the shop. It was Sunday and the shop would stay closed. It gave me the perfect opportunity to finish up dull paperwork. And, if I was being honest with myself, I also hoped to see Detective Briggs while I was on Harbor Lane. I hadn't spoken to him since I told him about the apparent affair between Tim and Charlene.

Lester was not usually open on Sunday, but I smelled the heavy scent of coffee as I reached my shop door. I hadn't seen him much all weekend and decided to stop in and say hello before starting paperwork.

I knocked on the front door and peered through the window to get his attention. Lester put down the coffee pot and came to the door to let me inside.

"I see you are working on Sunday too," I said. "I'm finally going to get to the paperwork I have piling up on my desk." I looked at his coffee station. It was covered with flavored syrups, cans of whipped cream and bits of chocolate. "I think your Sunday drudge work looks much more fun than mine."

"I'm trying out some new flavors, so you're just in time to do a little taste test. If you don't mind."

"Not at all. I could use another burst of caffeine. Yesterday was a long day . . . and night."

Lester walked behind his counter to his barista station. "I, for one, am glad to have this whole event behind us. With the crowds, the news crews, the unfortunate murder and that blasted window decorating contest, this past week seemed about a year long."

"I totally agree with that, Les. Elsie tells me you are remodeling your bathroom and putting in one of those fancy soak tubs."

"Yes. We just put in the drain last night. Looking forward to that tub too. Especially in the cold weather. My days as a firefighter have caught up to me. I can feel every joint and muscle these days." He poured some syrup into a cup and followed it with hot coffee. The aroma of coffee and vanilla filled the air.

"Smells good. What flavor is this?"

"This is my vanilla and peppermint surprise. Would you like a squirt of whipped cream?"

"The day I say no to that question is the day I've given up on all that is good in the world. So yes."

He chuckled as he topped the coffee with a creamy white swirl. He grabbed a handful of crushed peppermint and tossed it on top of the whipped cream.

He smiled proudly at his creation as he handed it to me.

I did what any self-respecting coffee taster would do and licked off some of the whipped cream and peppermint first. As always, the mint tickled my nose. I placed the cup quickly down on the counter to avoid tossing the coffee all over the store as I sneezed. Lester looked somewhat taken aback as I covered my nose. A sneeze chirped through the store.

"Bless you."

"Thanks. Peppermint makes me sneeze." I lowered my hand, but as I drew it away, another faint smell threaded through the rich aroma of coffee and the strong scent of peppermint. I lifted my hand to my face again.

"Another sneeze?" Lester asked. "I shouldn't have put the mint candies on top."

I shook my head. "No, it's not the candy. I smell something else." Poor Lester looked almost distraught as I rubbed my hand on the cup and brought my palm to my nose. "That's it. That's the same chemical odor I smelled on the victim's sweater."

Lester paled and his mouth dropped open.

"No, I know you didn't have anything to do with the murder, but there is something on this cup. It's faint, too faint for the normal nose." I reached my hand out. "Do you mind, Les? I think you might just have helped Detective Briggs' case."

The color returned to his face as he placed his hand in mine. I brought it closer to my nose. "It's on your hand. It's a strong chemical smell. It's exactly what I smelled on the sweater. Is it from something you use here in the coffee shop?"

Lester's fuzzy brows bunched together. "Gosh, I hope not. I don't think my customers would appreciate chemical odors with their coffees." He walked to his sink and carried over the sanitizer he used to wash his hands.

I took a deep whiff and shook my head. "That's not it."

"Thank goodness. I've been using that hand cleanser since I opened." He reached up and scratched his chin and then smelled his fingers. "I know exactly what it is." He lightly smacked the side of his head. "Of course. I must have washed my hands a dozen times last night to try and rid my hands of the odor. It's the adhesive my plumber friend and I used to stick together the pipes for the bathtub drain. The drain pipes are made of a special thick resin, and they require an adhesive to make a proper seal. It's quite odorous, as you noticed."

My sleuthing adrenaline kicked into gear, but I had to keep a lid on my excitement. Mostly because the direction my mind was heading still didn't make much sense. "Is this adhesive something that gets used a lot on a house construction site."

"If the homeowners are planning to have bathrooms, yes," he said with a light laugh.

"Good to know." I lifted my cocoa cup and raised it with a wink. "Thanks for the minty treat. It's delicious. And thanks for having smelly adhesive on your hands. You just solved a mystery for me."

# CHAPTER 33

My plan to muddle through paperwork was interrupted by the latest development in the Ruxley murder case. I sat down at my desk and pushed aside my work to write down everything we knew about the case so far. Or everything I knew. I hadn't seen Detective Briggs since the day before when he was leaving to ask Tim Ruxley about his relationship with Charlene. He'd mentioned that he'd be speaking to Randall Dayton too. Alibi or not, this last piece of evidence had me focused back on Dayton. I pulled out a blank sheet of paper from my printer and scribbled down a quick graphic. There was Timothy Ruxley, brother of the victim who had hardly spoken to Chad in years because of a falling out in the family business, a business Chad, his older brother, had inherited. Inheritance issues could sometimes create a lot of animosity between family members. It seemed that had been the case with the Ruxley brothers.

Timothy also appeared to have romantic feelings for Charlene Ruxley, Chad's ex-wife, and it seemed Chad never really got over losing her. But there was no connection between Tim and the two unexpected odors on the sweater and ribbon. Or at least none that we could find.

On the other hand, Charlene the ex-wife, who was romantically linked to Tim, had access to the same ribbon that was discovered around Chad's throat. She also had access to the trestle table that had the distinct odor of Douglas Fir, the same woodsy scent I smelled on the sweater and ribbon.

Then there was the third wheel on my three-wheeled diagram. Randall Dayton had a past with Chad Ruxley. Chad was instrumental in the collapse of Randall's father's business and indirectly responsible for his suicide. It seemed Randall had a much bigger motive than even the disgruntled brother or ex-wife. It was easy to connect Randall to both of the unique scents on Chad's clothing. He worked with a great deal of Douglas Fir lumber, and while there was no direct evidence of it yet, it was easy to assume that at some point he had been working with the adhesive for plumbing pipes. But there was a big hole in the Randall Dayton theory. The man couldn't have been in two places at once. It was the pancakes that should have taken him right out of the running, but something kept bringing me back to Dayton. I was missing something that was as obvious as the talented nose on my face. I just couldn't figure it out.

I decided to take a stroll around the shop to free my mind and, who was I kidding, procrastinate a few more minutes before starting paperwork. I walked to the big bay window where Ryder's magical display was slowly shrinking and drying. Even in its slightly deteriorated state, it was wonderful. I could have kicked myself for immediately confessing that Ryder had done the whole thing. Naturally, I didn't feel right taking even an ounce of credit, but at the same time, it might have been better to keep it to myself. At least until after the judging. Fortunately, Ryder took it in stride and didn't seem too disappointed in losing.

As I spun away from the window display, something popped into my head about that day. Tyler was helping Yolanda. I could recognize him because of the pungent sports cream he'd applied to his sore muscle. The night before, I saw Taylor and knew it was him because of the lack of medicinal smell. I had seen Randall Dayton three times.

The first time in the diner, I didn't notice any tobacco smell. Although I wished I had. It might have stopped Lola from even sharing a slice of pie with him. Then Lola complained that he smelled like smoke on their date. In the Corner Market, with the blonde, no tobacco smell. But last night with Kate, it was back.

Just maybe Randall Dayton *could* be in two places at once. I rushed back to my computer and spent the next few minutes typing in keywords and combing through the pages. I found the article about Big Bob Construction losing its license. As I read further, there was a mention of Bob's sons, Randall and Scott. I typed in both their names, and bingo, I found what I needed. Randall and Scott Dayton were identical twins. Randall followed in his father's footsteps and went into construction, but Scott had gone to Hollywood to try his luck in show business. It seemed he was mostly a commercial actor. One thing was for sure, the two brothers were as closely matched as Franki's boys. Only Randall and Scott were easy to tell apart because one smelled like tobacco and one did not. I wasn't completely sure which one was the smoker, but at this point, it didn't matter.

I stared down at the paperwork on my desk. It could wait. But the new information I had for Detective Briggs couldn't. I walked out to the sidewalk and stared down Harbor Lane. Detective Briggs' car was not parked out front. The black and white patrol car was gone too. Maybe Briggs had figured things out and he was already heading out to the site to find Dayton.

After I'd helped out on the murder case for Marian Fitch, Briggs had given me his direct line. I dialed the number and was disappointed that it went straight to voicemail. I left him a quick message to call me but didn't want to provide details over the phone. I hoped it wouldn't be long until he listened to his messages. It was Sunday and, in truth, I didn't know all that much about Briggs' social life, except that he rode a motorcycle and he didn't like crowds. It was possible he had been out late Saturday night, and he'd decided to unplug from work for the morning. And just exactly what was he doing out so late on Saturday night? I had to squash that thought right away before it led my imagination astray.

I was thoroughly disappointed that I couldn't reach him. So thoroughly that I was sure I couldn't possibly concentrate on paperwork. I decided to walk down to Franki's for breakfast while I waited for him to call me back.

# CHAPTER 34

*A*n angry looking storm loomed out over the ocean. The gulls that usually huddled on the pier in the morning waiting patiently for food crumbs and fish bits had moved inland. The birds always knew when it was time to clear the coastline for a storm. It was no wonder Kingston had tucked his beak back under his wing when I invited him along for the morning.

I could feel this one coming in my bones as well. The clouds were tall, reaching far up into the atmosphere, and they carried with them that dark, ominous glow of thunder, lightning and sheets of rain. The morning air was cold but not quite frigid enough for snow. That meant the blanket of snow on the town would be turned to mushy ice.

The depressingly gray sky, the eerie quiet left behind from the weekend's event and my sense that I had discovered the name of the murderer sent an odd chill through me that had nothing to do with the temperature.

Long before I reached the diner, I'd decided firmly on one of Franki's yogurt parfaits for breakfast. Her parfait was a whispery light concoction of vanilla honey yogurt, berries and Franki's homemade pecan granola. After the very irresponsible dinner of mashed potatoes, macaroni and cheese and caramel cake, I needed to eat something nutritious or risk feeling like a soft potato myself. I could almost feel the heavy starches weighing me down as I walked through the diner parking lot.

Most of the town had been out late last night, and there were only a few cars and one work truck in the parking lot. I didn't give the work truck a second glance as I walked past it until the diner door opened and Randall Dayton walked out. Or was it Scott? Or was I totally wrong about all of it?

Dayton was alone. He had just finished a phone call as he stepped off the curb to walk around to the driver's side of the truck. Rude jerk that he was, he took a moment to look me up and down. Then he pulled the keys from his pocket.

I didn't know if it was the way he'd so brazenly looked at me or if it was the way he'd treated Lola but my anger made me blurt out the words before I could give them careful thought.

"I must be seeing double," I said with a forced laugh.

He stopped halfway along the driver's side and turned back to me, his dark brow arched in suspicion. The work truck led me to believe that I was talking to Randall. There was no tobacco smell.

"Excuse me?" The harsh way he said the words should have given me pause, but I forged right ahead.

"It's just that I've been seeing you so much this weekend. It's almost as if there are two of you. Identical twins, I assume."

His face grew red with agitation. He glanced around, it seemed to make sure no one could hear me exposing the truth. His angry scowl shot across the street to the Port Danby Police Station. There were still no cars out front.

"You're that woman who was snooping around at the murder scene."

"So you were there watching? Interesting. Well, have a good day." I tried to walk past him but quickly found I'd made a terrible mistake in taunting a murderer.

It took me a stunned second to realize that he had wrapped his hand around my arm. He smothered my scream with his other ice cold hand. My moment of extreme terror was cut short by a sharp pain in my head. A layer of darkness swept over me.

My eyes opened and my head thudded with pain. My first thoughts were to climb out of bed and go down the hallway to the medicine cabinet for aspirin, but when my bottom was suddenly launched into the air before smacking a car seat, my aching head cleared and the terror returned.

I reached instinctively for the door handle, even knowing full well that we were racing along Highway 48 at full speed. The handle was locked. I frantically rubbed my fingers over the window button, not knowing what I would do once I got it open. But it seemed I wouldn't need to decide that either. The window was locked.

"Don't know why they put child safety buttons on a work truck. This is the first time I've ever had to use them." Randall Dayton stared straight ahead. From the side he had a jutting forehead and chin that made him look horribly mean. And, it seemed that he wasn't just mean but a murderer. Apparently Dash had good instincts when it came to judging people. He'd sensed something was wrong with Dayton right away.

I'd been knocked unconscious long enough for him to push me into his truck and head for the highway. I reached up and winced as my fingers grazed the tender lump on the back of my head. "Ouch, what did you hit me with?"

Dayton lifted his hand from the steering wheel and curled it into a menacing fist. "I'm an amateur boxer. You went down even faster than Ruxley."

The sky darkened with the impending storm, and the first drop of icy rain plinked off the windshield of his truck. He took a sharp left. The truck tires left the ground for a second as we flew onto the road that led to Beacon Cliffs. My captor didn't bother to belt me in, and I had to grab the edge of the seat to keep from being pitched into the dashboard.

"Where are you taking me?"

He stared ahead and drove with one arm casually draped over the steering wheel as if he was just taking a drive in the country.

"You won't get away with this. Detective Briggs was expecting me this morning." I kept my voice steady, not wanting him to know that I was scared to death. "He'll come looking for me."

Dayton looked over at me. He had a truly unlikable, cold face. What on earth was Lola thinking? "I doubt he'll come straight to Beacon Cliffs. Seems to me I've got more than enough time to get rid of his nosy little assistant long before he figures out you're missing."

My head hurt but it had cleared completely. I was thinking straighter. I discretely reached into my coat pocket. My shoulders dropped in despair when I found that it was empty.

"I dumped your phone back on the highway."

I had definitely pushed my nose out too far this time. Briggs would lecture me for taking such a chance. That thought made my throat tighten. What if he never got the chance to lecture me? Dayton had already killed one person, seemingly without an ounce of regret.

"You killed Chad Ruxley because he caused your family terrible grief. I understand that. But I haven't done anything to you."

"Nope, you haven't, and if you had kept your nose out of things and not uncovered the truth about my twin brother, you wouldn't have opened your big mouth this morning and you'd be sitting in that diner right now enjoying a plate of pancakes."

I scooted back and faced out the side window. "I was going to order a yogurt parfait. And two murders will just mean double the prison sentence." I turned back to him. "For each of you, since you are both going to be charged with the murder of Chad Ruxley. I take it you're the builder."

"Yes, I am."

The punch of adrenaline had me convinced I could somehow talk my way out of getting killed. Or maybe it was just helping me avoid thinking about my inevitable fate.

"I guess it was your brother who took my friend, Lola, out on a date to secure you an alibi. Obviously, he is far more charming than you because she enjoyed the date."

"We both do just fine with the ladies."

"Can't imagine how," I sneered back. I decided to get all the details

I could in case I was lucky enough to survive this. It seemed I really was a detective at heart. "I guess this whole thing was planned. The Holiday Light Flotilla is an annual event, so you knew exactly where Chad Ruxley's boat would be this weekend. How did you manage to line up your work timetable with the flotilla?"

"Easy enough. I told the clients that I couldn't start until the end of November. That way I knew we'd still be in town for the boat show. Scott came into town last week, but we made sure never to be in the same place at the same time. So no one, not even my crew, knew he was around. Your friend smiled at me in the diner. I knew I'd found my alibi."

I really needed to talk to Lola about her indiscriminate flirting. I only hoped I would get that chance.

I grasped the edge of the seat as Dayton pulled the truck off onto an unpaved stretch of road, or, to be more precise, a cleared section of forest. A lush evergreen forest acted like a natural wall between the exclusive neighborhood of Beacon Cliffs and the treacherously steep cliffs along the coast. It seemed we were heading into the forest and away from any chance of being seen.

That earlier punch of adrenaline started feeling more like a punch in the stomach. I felt slightly nauseous as it occurred to me we were heading toward the highly insufficient safety fence constructed to keep people from slipping over the side of the cliffs to the jagged rocks below.

"You won't get away with this, you monster."

"I think I will. You are the only person who knows about my brother being in town. We had this planned down to every last detail. It's taken a few years to get things lined up, but there was no way that plumber was going to get away with destroying our family. I'd planned on rowing out to his boat to strangle him but then luck went my way. I spotted his ex-wife with the singers and I noticed they'd left all their gear unattended. It was easy enough to grab her phone to text Ruxley. There was an extra piece of ribbon in the bag and I took it, deciding I'd found the perfect person to frame."

"Maybe if your dad had run his business properly, with safety rules followed, none of it would have happened."

I knew I was tossing gasoline on a fire, but I couldn't help myself. I wanted Dayton to know that Ruxley had done the right thing and that he didn't deserve to die. Just as I wanted Dayton to know that he was a wretched human being.

"Like you, Ruxley was sticking his nose in other people's business. He deserved what he got." His hands tightened on the steering wheel as he spoke. A chill went through me as I pictured those same hands pulling the ribbon tight around Ruxley's neck. Would he do the same to me?

"My brother has a part as an extra on a movie set just two hours away. It's one of those disaster movies with a big crowd on the streets watching as their town is destroyed by meteors. His name is on the roster, but it was easy enough for him to slip away unnoticed. He came into town just for the date I'd arranged with your friend. He left a few hours later and was back on the set the next morning. So our alibis are tight, and your life is, unfortunately, going to be cut short."

My confusion was replaced quickly with clarity. The poor stooge had apparently trusted his brother to leave town as planned. Only it seemed the very attractive Kate Yardley hadn't been part of the plan.

Dayton pulled the truck between some trees and stopped a good twenty yards from the fencing that separated me from a terrible death on sharp rocks. My time was running short. Since he outweighed me by a good hundred pounds, it seemed my best bet was to throw him off mentally. And he had just provided me with exactly what I needed to destroy his cocky confidence. He was sure that once he was rid of me, he would get away with murder.

"It's a shame your brother is a smoker. He should follow your example."

He cast a suspicious glower at me. "What are you talking about?"

"The reason I was snooping around the murder scene is because Detective Briggs calls me to assist. I have hyperosmia, which, in layman's terms, means I can smell a pine needle from ten feet away. I can detect the slightest odor on clothing and on murder ribbons. Like the smell of fresh cut lumber or the pungent scent of adhesive used in construction."

His expression darkened. I was getting to him, only it seemed I was just pushing myself into greater danger. But I hadn't delivered the final blow.

"You're bluffing."

"Am I?" I even managed a fake grin. "Those pieces of evidence will point Detective Briggs in the right direction, even after I'm gone." I only wished I'd found out what the adhesive smell was before this morning. Then I could have let Briggs know. At least my evil captor didn't know the truth. "Of course, I didn't really need a super power nose to smell tobacco on your brother's clothing because it's such a strong, foul smell. Anyone can detect it. Even in cold weather, like last night on the pier when I saw your brother out with one of the local women."

Dayton's thick forehead and heavy brow had dropped so low over his eyes, I could barely see them. What I could see plainly was the deep red color of anger rising up above the collar of his shirt.

Heavy rain drops began to pelt the windshield. The first flashes of lightning were followed by gusts of wind.

"What are you talking about? My brother left town Thursday night." His fists curled, and I questioned whether I should continue. His confidence had been erased. It seemed I'd genuinely thrown him off his game, but at the same time, his entire body was tense with anger.

I'd gone this far, and I had nothing to lose.

"No, he didn't. In fact, I was in the market on Saturday afternoon. You two just missed each other by an hour."

His mouth stretched into a thin angry line. It was obvious he remembered seeing me at the store. He fished around in his coat for his phone and pulled it out. I could hear the light ring of the phone on the other side followed by a recorded message.

"Hey, it's me. Call me back as soon as you get this." He shoved the phone back into his pocket. "You might be the only person that noticed there were two of us. Either way, you're going head first over that cliff." He climbed out of the truck.

I lunged over the console, fell into the driver's seat and grabbed for the door handle. I pushed the door open and jumped out into the cold, wet wind. I didn't get more than three steps before he had me in his grasp again.

# CHAPTER 35

*I*t was hard to see anything in the blinding rain. The storm had moved in quickly, and it wasted no time in wreaking havoc on the shoreline. I kept my face averted from the onslaught of icy rain as Dayton pulled me along toward the cliffs. His boot hit a jutting tree root. He stumbled forward but managed to keep a firm grasp on my arm. Even through the thick layers of my coat and sweater, I could feel his fingers leaving a bruise.

The near stumble made one thing clear. Dayton couldn't see any better than me in the storm. In that regard, at least, we were at an equal disadvantage. It was my only chance.

I kept my bleary gaze glued to the ground to look for an opportunity. Then, after a morning that had gone horribly wrong, a sprinkle of luck came my way. We came to a thick, knotted tree root just as Dayton's phone rang in his pocket. I was sure he would ignore it, but he yanked it out, ready to lay into his brother for messing up the plan. "Is that you?" he barked into the phone. "Where are you?"

Dayton was temporarily distracted by the phone call. I whipped my arm free and shoved him hard with both hands. The heels of his boots got caught on the jutting tree root and his arms flailed in the air as he fell backward. As badly I would have liked to see the man fall hard as a stone on his backside, I raced off into the trees.

The storm clouds and the tall trees had blotted out any trace of daylight. The deeper I went into the trees, the darker it got. And there was nothing I hated more than the dark. But as much as I feared it, I was more afraid of the tall, vengeful monster I'd just escaped from.

I'd lost sight of Dayton, but I had no doubt he wasn't far behind. Rainwater dripped off of me as if I was standing fully clothed beneath an ice cold shower. My teeth chattered from the cold and from fear. The trees were an excellent place to hide, but I badly needed to get to the road and find some form of help.

I headed in the direction of Beacon Cliffs. Just as I stepped out from the thickest patch of trees, a streak of lightning flashed above, illuminating the entire forest and surrounding neighborhood with nature's biggest and brightest spotlight. Before the glow dimmed, my gaze swept behind me. My heart jumped right into my throat as I caught a glimpse of Dayton lumbering through the trees and heading straight for me.

I would never make it clear of the forest and out to the neighborhood without him grabbing me first. I had no choice except to turn back to the trees and hide.

The forest loam became soft as pudding as I raced between the trees and shrubs. Thunder rumbled overhead, vibrating the ground beneath my feet and shaking my resolve even more. I searched around in the shadows for the biggest tree and managed to dash behind it just before the next streak of lightning.

I huddled behind the trunk of the tree and tried hard to listen for any sound that might signal Dayton was getting close, but I couldn't hear anything through the wind, rain and thunder. Rivulets of rainwater began rushing through the forest, carrying debris off and over the edge of the cliff. I shuddered thinking how close I'd come to being thrown off that cliff. And I shuddered again reminding myself that I was still not out of danger. Far from it. And that frightening revelation was followed by the tiniest sound, the snap of a branch being broken under foot.

Dayton's angry, terrifying face peered around the tree trunk. A scream caught in my throat as I stumbled back. His hand reached out and grabbed my arm.

"I'm tired of this of game of hide and seek," he sneered. But his growling expression faded suddenly. His eyes widened and looked as if they might pop from his head.

"That's too bad. I hear hide and seek is sort of a favorite in the state penitentiary." Detective Briggs stepped out from behind Dayton, revealing that he was holding a gun to the man's head. "Only, in jail, I think you'll be the one hiding."

Seconds later, red flashing lights lit up the rain soaked forest. "Over here," Briggs called through the trees.

Four Chesterton police officers emerged through the shadowy foliage. They reached us and Briggs handed off Dayton. "Get this guy out of my sight." The officers took over from there. The cold, the exhaustion and the terror had finally caught up to me. My knees turned to jelly and I collapsed right into Detective Briggs' arms.

"I've got you," he said in a deep, soothing tone that instantly made the fear drain away. I knew I was safe.

It took me a few seconds to gather my wits. As much as I wanted to stay tucked there in the security of his arms, I straightened, letting him know I was fine.

Briggs reached up and pushed a long strand of wet hair off my face. I couldn't stop gazing at him. He was even handsome soaking wet.

"How did you find me?" I finally managed to sputter.

"You can thank Franki for that."

The rain dripped off the brim of his hat. He reached for my arm and led me back through the trees. "I headed into the office to look for my phone. It had dropped out of my coat pocket on my way out of the station last night."

"I tried to call you this morning, but it went straight to voicemail."

"It needed to be charged. What timing. That phone couldn't have jumped from my pocket at a worse time, it seems. Everything would have turned out differently." He stopped, and for the first time I'd ever seen, he was visibly shaken. "Lacey, I'm so sorry this happened."

His pained expression of regret and his words went right to my chest. "It was my fault. I shouldn't have stuck my neck out so far. I saw Dayton and I teased him about having a twin."

Briggs turned his head sharply, flicking drops of rain off of his hat. "You knew about the twin too?"

"Figured it out this morning, after I discovered the chemical smell on Ruxley's sweater was the adhesive contractors use for plumbing."

"That'll be just one more piece of evidence. Although this case looks pretty solid now."

We stepped out of the trees and into the clearing. I couldn't wait to get into his dry car. The Chesterton officers already had the suspect in their car. I couldn't even glance Dayton's direction. I was sure his mean face would haunt my nightmares for months to come.

"I still don't understand. What did Franki have to do with this?" I asked.

"She saw my car pull up to the station and ran across the street to find me. She was beyond despair and could hardly get the words out. She said she was taking an order and saw you walking across the parking lot, heading for the diner. She wrote down the order and then looked up and you were gone. You had never stepped foot inside the diner. All she saw was Dayton's truck speeding out of the parking lot. She knew something was wrong, so she came over to let me know."

Briggs opened the car door. I squinted into the wind. "I'm soaking wet," I reminded him.

He reached up and placed a gloved finger beneath my chin to stop it from trembling. "And freezing. The car seats will dry. Besides, we need to protect Samantha from a bad cold." He tapped my nose. "She's critical to our case." I slipped into the passenger seat and was instantly relieved to be in a dry, warm place and away from the biting, wet wind.

Briggs leaned down. "I'll be right back."

I reached up and wiped away the condensation on the passenger window and watched him as he talked to the police officers. His slightly long hair was soaking wet as it curled up on the back of his coat collar. I hugged my arms around myself trying to squeeze away the trembling in my body. If not for Franki and Briggs, the morning might have ended very badly.

Briggs walked back to the car and climbed into the driver's seat. He started the motor and cranked up the heater.

I smiled over at him and realized my face was nearly numb from the cold. "Samantha, eh?"

He turned his car toward the road. "You always do that little twitching movement when you're trying to uncover a scent."

"Yes, it helps wake up the olfactory cells."

"It reminds me of that old, old show, Bewitched. Samantha wiggled her nose when she was about to perform magic."

I sat back and thought about the name. "You know something? I like it. And I can shorten it to Sam."

The silence of relief washed over us as we headed back to the highway.

"Miss Pinkerton," he said quietly.

"Yes, Detective Briggs?"

"Don't ever scare me like that again."

"I promise."

# CHAPTER 36

The Annual Holiday Light Flotilla was gone, but the events of the weekend would stay with us, and most especially me, for a long time. I would eventually have to testify in court about my 'kidnapping', a word Detective Briggs used in a report and a word that really brought home how serious things had been. I wasn't sure if the incident would douse my curiosity or love for a good mystery, but in the future I planned to be just a little less bold when I knew someone was a cold blooded murderer. Once I'd revealed the entire story to Lola, she understood how lucky she was that she'd come through it all unharmed. She insisted she would be much more picky in the future, but just like with my plan to be less bold, we both still had to prove ourselves.

I had arranged a red rose and white lily holiday bouquet for Franki, and Elsie helped me make a small gift batch of chocolate truffles for Detective Briggs. They were ridiculously simple gestures for two people who'd saved my life.

I carried the flowers into the diner. As usual, Franki was busy on the floor, but she stopped for a second to come over and greet me as I placed the bouquet next to the cash register.

"Oh my goodness, Lacey, it's beautiful. It really brightens up this place."

I shook my head and swallowed to relieve the tightness in my throat. I hadn't expected to get emotional, but the second I saw her smile, I was overwhelmed with gratitude. "This place is already bright because of you." I hugged her quickly to not let her see the tears in my eyes. "Thank you," I said quietly.

She hugged me back just as tightly. I realized, in that moment, that I was no longer a newcomer in town. I had found a true home in Port Danby.

I released her and took a steadying breath. "I'll let you go. Just wanted to get these flowers to you."

"They are lovely, and I'm just glad you're all right."

We hugged again, and I walked out of the diner with my gift bag of truffles. Detective Briggs' car was out front. I was sure he was in his office working on the lengthy report for the case.

I walked inside. It was still early. Hilda was not behind her desk. The black and white patrol car was not out front, so Officer Chinmoor was out and about.

Hilda always left a bell on the counter when she wasn't at her desk. I rang it. Seconds later, Detective Briggs emerged from his office.

"You look rested," I said. "I mean you always look fairly relaxed for someone who has your job, but you look even more so today. I'll bet you're glad to have this case behind you."

"I sure am." He walked out to greet me. "How are you doing?"

I smiled. "Thanks to you, I'm alive. So I guess I'm doing pretty well." I held up the bag. "I made you chocolate truffles." I tilted my head side to side. "Actually, I helped Elsie make you truffles."

He took the bag and looked inside. "These look delicious, but you didn't need to go through the trouble. It's my job to keep Port Danby citizens safe."

I nodded. "Yes, I know. I was just a Port Danby citizen who got herself in too deep with a murder case. You would have done it for anyone. Enjoy the chocolates." I turned to walk out.

"I probably wouldn't have been scared out of my wits though," he added.

I turned around. He stepped a bit closer.

"I was scared to death that something might happen to you. I was so relieved to see you standing behind that tree, Lacey."

"Not as relieved as I was to see you standing behind that murderer."

His lopsided smile kicked up on the side of his mouth. He lifted his face and peered up. My gaze followed his. We were standing right beneath the cluster of mistletoe.

"Do you think that little plant really has kissing power?" I asked.

"Might be only one way to prove it."

My heart sped up as he leaned closer.

"It's cold as a polar bear's nose out there," Officer Chinmoor blurted as he burst into the station, bringing with him a sweep of frigid air. Briggs straightened again. I was shocked at how disappointed I was that I wasn't going to get that kiss.

I pointed behind me. "Well, I better get to the shop."

"Thank you for the chocolates, Miss Pinkerton."

"Have a good day, Detective Briggs."

# MELT-IN-YOUR-MOUTH CHOCOLATE TRUFFLES

*View online at: www.londonlovett.com/recipe-box/*

# Melt-in-Your-Mouth
## CHOCOLATE TRUFFLES

### Ingredients:

1 lb quality milk chocolate

1/2 lb quality semi-sweet chocolate

3/4 cup heavy whipping cream

1 tsp vanilla

1/4 tsp salt

### Directions:

1. Add vanilla, salt and whipping cream to a large bowl. Beat until cream is whipped into the soft peak stage.

2. Coarsely chop 1/2 lb milk chocolate and 1/4 lb semi-sweet chocolate.

3. **Set up a double boiler** for melting the chocolate.

-If you don't have a double boiler you can use a glass bowl resting on top of a large pot on the stove. Fill the pot partially with water, and rest the glass bowl on top. (*Be sure the bottom of the glass bowl is not touching the water in the base pot*).

4. Add the chopped chocolate to the glass bowl and use low heat to slowly melt the chocolate. Be careful to not let the chocolate get too hot or burn, and stir often. Avoid getting any water in the chocolate bowl.

5. Once the chocolate is melted, remove the glass bowl from heat and let cool for a few minutes.

6. After the melted chocolate has cooled some, gently fold in the whipped cream.

7. Cover the bowl with plastic wrap and place in the refrigerator to set. Filling should be solid enough to roll into balls and hold its shape. It will take about 2 hours in the fridge.

8. Line a large cookie sheet with wax or parchment paper.

9. **Shape the chocolate.** Scoop a heaping teaspoon of filling and gently roll it into a ball shape. (The shape won't be perfect, and it doesn't need to be.) Work quickly and touch the filling as little as possible--it will start melting from the heat of your fingers. Place the balls onto the prepared cookie sheet, and refrigerate for at least one hour.

10. **Prepare the coating chocolate.**

-Grate about 2oz of the milk chocolate (I used a cheese grater) and set aside.

-Coarsely chop the remaining milk chocolate and 1/4 lb semi-sweet chocolate.

-Repeat the double broiler steps from the filling preparation and melt the coating chocolate.

11. Let the melted chocolate cool slightly.

12. Pour half of the melted chocolate onto a smooth, clean surface. (ex: a granite countertop or a flat cookie sheet)

13. Use a metal spatula to spread the melted chocolate back and forth on the work surface. Sprinkle on some grated chocolate to temper it and move the chocolate around until the grated chocolate is melted in.

14. Once the chocolate is cooled to room temperature, drop a filling ball into the coating chocolate and roll around to coat as quickly as possible. Touch it as little as possible in this step as well. Set back onto the tray lined with wax or parchment paper. Top with sprinkles if desired.

15. Repeat until all chocolate balls are coated.

16. Place the tray of finished truffles in a cool, dry place to harden. *Don't put them in the refrigerator because the moisture in the fridge will cause a white cast on the outer coating.

17. Enjoy!

# ABOUT THE AUTHOR

London Lovett is the author of the new Port Danby Cozy Mystery series. She loves getting caught up in a good mystery and baking delicious new treats! (The recipes from each book are available on www.londonlovett.com/recipe-box)

Subscribe to London's newsletter on her website to never miss an update.

https://www.londonlovett.com/
londonlovettwrites@gmail.com